Lynd

DECLAN

HOLLISTER

KRIS MICHAELS

Happy Reading!

Kris Michaels

CHAPTER 1

Note: Declan's book starts immediately after Zeke's book stops. For those who read Sage's story, that book is set in the future, after this story. Sage is still at Hollister for this story.

DECLAN HOWARD WIPED down the bar one last time, then threw his towel into the dirty towel bin. He'd wash them tomorrow before the bar opened. But tonight, now that his sister's surprise engagement party had ended, he had someone waiting for him.

Walking back to the office to grab his keys, he smiled as he thought about her. Melody was one of the few women he'd been with more than once. He'd been with her more than any woman he'd hooked up with. She was a sexy, fun, wild thing, and no one else measured up. Hell, he'd even considered a run at a monogamous relationship for her, but she'd let him know up front that what they were doing was for fun only.

Fun was good for him. Not exactly what he wanted anymore, but he'd take it. As he grabbed the keys from his desk and tossed them into the air, the jingle of bells at the front door made him frown and hustle back to the main part of the bar. The town was tucked in for the night. Hell, the boardwalks outside the buildings rolled themselves up by ten o'clock on the weekend. Whoever was there probably wasn't local.

The stranger standing at the bar confirmed his suspicion. "Hey, we're closing, but I can get you a beer," Declan said, making a point to look at his watch. "Fifteen minutes, then I have to head out."

The man stared at him before shaking his head. "I'm looking for Declan Howard."

A tendril of uneasiness trickled down his spine. "Yeah? What do you need with him?"

The man spun to look at the bar before turning back to Declan. "Do you know him?"

"Better than anyone else."

"Do you think he'd be interested in selling the bar?" The stranger leaned against the bar and stared at him.

Declan made a show of thinking before shaking his head. "This here bar is his primary income. I don't think he'd sell." Declan wouldn't get rid of the Bit and Spur if offered a million dollars. His little bar was his connection to the town and its people. Hell, he wouldn't even know what to do with a million dollars. Not like he could ranch or anything. He liked animals, but he didn't want to ranch. It wasn't in his blood like it was in the people around here.

"Do you know when he'll be in?" the stranger asked. "I'd like to ask him for myself."

"Tomorrow. He's here every day." Declan leaned against the back bar. "Pretty sure you'd be wasting your time."

The man rolled his eyes. "I'll take that up with the owner." He knocked on the bar with one fist and walked out. Declan sized him up as he exited. The jeans were new, and so were the boots. But the guy didn't wear them right. Like he was a drugstore cowboy or one of those city types who wanted to go to a country western bar for the night and fit in—or, at least, try to.

Whatever. Declan would deal with the stranger tomorrow. Tonight, he had other plans. Declan made another pass through the Bit to make sure everything was shut down and locked up, unplugging everything that didn't have to be plugged in. He'd heard too many horror stories about fires starting from faulty wiring on small appliances. He used the best breaker strips and had a state-of-the-art fire suppression system installed. It had taken six months of profits, but this business was his pride and joy.

Locking the door behind him, Declan circled to the back of the bar where his truck was parked. Unlike the locals, he locked his truck. The last time he didn't, a drunk cowboy had climbed in and passed out, thinking it was his. Unfortunately, before Declan had closed for the night, that cowboy had puked in his truck. Twice.

Never again.

He started up and headed out of the parking lot. There were no other vehicles he could see on the highway heading north, so the man who'd come in looking to buy the bar must have headed south toward Belle. Declan shook his head again.

An offer to buy his bar out of the blue like that was unusual, for sure. It wasn't like Hollister was a booming metropolis. They had a population of almost four hundred people. The town had grown with the things going on at the Marshall ranch. Which absolutely no one talked about. Frank Marshall was damn good to the town. He and Andrew Hollister Senior were the two mainstays in the area. They provided jobs and assistance when people needed it. Nah, the people in Hollister knew where their bread was buttered. They weren't going to mess that up. He smiled as he drove. God, he'd missed Mel. *Where had she been?*

He hadn't seen her in a couple of months. She was a firecracker, and he was stuck on her pretty hard there for a while. If she hadn't disappeared, he would have asked her out on a real date, which was something he never did. He hadn't even taken a woman home since Mel fell out of sight. Partly because he was tired of the anonymous sex. Partly because they didn't tick his boxes like Melody had. Maybe he was getting picky in his old age. He snorted. More like he was getting old in his old age. He actually had been thinking about finding someone special. Someone to be semi-permanent

in his life. Permanent could wait, but he was …
lonely. Declan rolled his eyes at himself. "Get over
yourself." He chuckled and turned up the radio.
Tonight, he wouldn't be lonely, and he'd have to
settle for that.

* * *

MELODY SAT IN HER TRUCK. Her home, actually,
and stared at the little house where she and Declan
had had some fantastic sex. It was more than that
for her, but she'd been warned Declan was a
player, and if she tried to corner him, he'd dump
her like red hot coals. She still came back time
after time. Declan was an elixir with a magic
combination of ingredients. His good looks and
skill in bed aside, the man packed a fun personality
and a caring nature inside that awesome shell.
Altogether, he was the man every girl who went to
that bar wanted and tried to get. She'd left with
him the first time she'd met him.

That night was ah-mazing. The sexual gymnas-
tics and fevered pace were borderline frantic and
one hundred percent phenomenal. She was
hooked on Declan Howard. She shook her head.
She was also a fool and, as happenstance would

have it, probably the luckiest unlucky person ever born.

Mel took a sip of water and stared at the house. How did she tell him? She'd practiced so many different ways. She knew what he'd say, and she was prepared for it. He didn't need to help out for several reasons. She rubbed her head, imagining the look on his face. The way his blond eyebrows would knit together. She'd seen that look before when he was about to step in to break up a fight or keep a guy from harassing a girl.

Still, she promised herself that no matter what happened tonight—no matter what Declan's response was, acceptance or, more than likely, a strong rejection—everything would be all right. She'd find a way to manage. She saw the headlights of a vehicle coming down the drive.

She should take the direct approach. Maybe. Or perhaps hint at what should already be obvious. Her mind raced as his truck parked next to hers. Finally, he was at her window. Her heart was beating so loudly in her chest as the fear of what she needed to do escalated to a tenor she expected but couldn't prepare for. It was time.

* * *

DECLAN TURNED into his drive and drove around the pothole he needed to fill. He'd take care of that on Sunday or Monday. His two days off a week unless there was some sort of celebration. Then he'd open up the bar and let whoever needed the space use it. As he drove down the driveway, he caught the taillights of Mel's truck.

He pulled in beside her and was startled to see her sitting inside. Getting out, he headed to her driver's side door and opened the door, reaching in for her hand. "Hey, beautiful. You could have waited inside. I didn't lock the door." Once he'd helped her out of her truck, he pulled her in for a kiss. She slipped into his arms, but he didn't feel the usual fire. He lifted his head. "What's wrong."

"Can we talk inside?" She motioned to the house.

"Sure." Declan walked beside her, holding her hand. He opened the door and let her in.

"May I use your bathroom?" Mel asked.

"Yeah, of course. You know where it is." Declan turned on the kitchen light, then opened the refrigerator and grabbed a beer. He didn't drink while behind the bar, so having a beer when he got home was a routine and an indulgence. He popped the top and took a swig before pulling one out for Melody.

A few moments later, she made her way back to the kitchen where he was. "Thanks, but no thanks." She waved off the beer.

Declan lifted an eyebrow. "So, what's up?"

"Can we sit down?" Melody said, motioning to the kitchen table and chairs.

Declan nodded and pulled a chair out for her, then sat down and stared at her. Her long wavy hair was pulled to one side and fell over her ample breasts. She was on the tall side for a woman, probably five foot nine or ten. Slender in the right places and curvy where it mattered. Her smile was almost a sensual experience. But she wasn't smiling tonight.

"Spill it." Declan took a long drink of his beer because he had a horrible feeling he knew where this shit was going.

"I'm going to need a job." Mel looked up at him. "I lost mine. Quit it, actually. I couldn't do what the management wanted me to do. It was … wrong."

Declan's eyebrows found and pinned themselves to the kitchen ceiling. So not what he expected to hear. "Um … okay." He leaned forward. "What can you do?"

"Ha!" Mel's blurt sounded more like a cry than a laugh. "Not much right now and even less later. But I can wait tables and pour drafts. I'm good with numbers, too. I could keep the books."

Declan sat back. "You want a job at the Bit?" Wow, that kind of slapped him in the face. Why hadn't he thought of that? Because he had a rule. No messing with the staff. Friendly, but a boss-and-employee relationship. Not what he wanted with Mel.

Mel sighed, and her shoulders dropped. "Declan. There's so much to tell you. First, I'm pregnant."

No way. He'd wrapped up every time they were together. He'd never had sex without a condom. Was he a dad? No, no … hell. What would Stephanie think? Fuck, he was screwed. He needed a paternity test. Pregnant? Condoms weren't a hundred percent. Well, shit. He'd never thought of himself as a father, and there he was, staring at that thought like a deer staring at a set of headlights. At that point, he had no idea what they would do next or what she expected from him. All sorts of thoughts ran through his mind: money concerns, work, and a family. How did he balance those things? Shit, how in the hell could he be a dad? But was the baby his? Was it? Hell, they weren't exclusive. Well, he wasn't. Surely, he wasn't the only one she'd been with. She was so damn hot and a wild one in bed. All those thoughts swirled together in an instant and were pushed to the side. Melody needed help. He could help. He could give her a job. But ...

Declan stared at her as his mind rebooted. "Okay ... and ..." He rubbed his face. "You think the baby's mine?"

Mel shrugged her shoulders in reply.

Declan blinked rapidly. "What does that mean?"

"I've been with you and one other man. He was right after we started hooking up, and I haven't been with him since. He used a condom, too."

"How far along are you?"

She shrugged again. "About four months, I think."

"You haven't been to the doctor?"

Tears formed in Mel's eyes. "No. I think I was in denial. I did the home pregnancy tests after I'd already quit my job."

"But you haven't been around for what? Two months?"

"Six weeks." Mel nodded. "I went home. I went back to Denver for a while. My mom and her boyfriend don't have much and suggested I come back here."

"To hit me up for child support," Declan finished for her. "Fuck."

"I'm not going to do that. I need a job. I don't expect anything from you or the other man. This baby is my responsibility. Not yours." Mel stood up. "This was a mistake. I'll look somewhere else for a job. Thanks for your time."

"Wait, Mel … Melody." She stopped at the front door. "If that is my baby, he or she *is* as much my responsibility as yours." Declan walked over to her. "Come on. You've had a hot minute to deal with this news. Dropping a bomb on me and then leaving won't do anything for either of us. Come sit down on the couch. I'm grabbing another beer. Do you want anything to drink?"

"Water, please." Mel shut the front door and walked over to his couch. "You have a couch?"

Declan laughed as he got the water and beer out of his refrigerator. "Yeah. We kind of bypassed this room when we were here, didn't we?"

"Yeah."

He handed her the water bottle and sat on the opposite side of the couch. "So … I used condoms, and so did the other man."

She nodded. "Something didn't work. I'm not Mary, and this isn't an immaculate conception."

Declan laughed. God help him; he laughed even though the situation was anything but funny. Mel had a way of dropping one-liners that set him off.

"I'm so sorry, Declan. I'll go down to Belle and try to find a job. When the baby is born, I'll get a test done. I don't have insurance, so doing one before he or she is born is too damn expensive. I looked into it." Mel picked at the label on her bottle of water.

"Just …" Declan sighed. "Let's not do anything rash. Okay? I can hire you at the Bit. I have insurance, and I can get you covered. The pay wouldn't be much." He stared at her. "Where are you staying?" He took a swig of his beer.

"In my truck right now."

Inhaling beer down your lungs was not wise. Fuck. Mel slid over and whapped him on the back several times as he choked on America's finest. He lifted his hand and took a couple of breaths before asking, "Excuse me?"

"There are no places for rent in Hollister or Buffalo. Belle thinks highly of their property, and I can't afford the rent if I want to eat." She looked down at her nails, which were no longer the long fancy type you got at a salon. They were filed down and natural. "I don't want a handout, Declan. But I can't ask for my old job back either." A tear slipped down her cheek.

Fuck him sideways. He reached over and wiped the tear away. "Why?" He had a few things spinning in his mind, and he needed time to shaft the wheat from the husk.

Mel sighed. "Because of you."

Declan's mind broke again. That made it the second or third time that night, didn't it? He put his beer on the floor by the couch and pulled off his boots, sitting them beside the couch. Then he picked up his beer and leaned back.

Mel kicked off her boots and pulled her knees up to her chin. She stared at him while he tried to put his mind back online. He wasn't having much luck.

"Aren't you going to ask why?"

Declan looked over at the beautiful woman who may or may not be carrying his child. The one who was living in her truck. The one who needed a job and insurance and said she'd quit her last job … because of him. "I'm not sure I can handle any more revelations tonight."

Mel dropped her eyes and traced the pattern of

the couch material with her nail. "This guy hired me as his receptionist. Except there were no customers. I played solitaire for weeks on end. He rarely came to the office. When he did, it was a huge whirlwind, and then he was gone."

"What kind of company?"

"A land company. He said he was a broker. He was fixated on this corner of South Dakota and Wyoming. He's trying to find as much land around here as he can. The only real work I did for him was to scan the real estate listings for this area once a day."

"Why does he want land? The Hollisters or Marshalls own almost everything around here."

"He never said, but I overheard a phone call on one of his rare days in the office. He was apologizing and assuring someone he'd be able to get more land. Two weeks later, he asked if I'd do some leg work for him. He sent me to Hollister to dig up any information I could on Declan Howard and Phil Granger."

Declan closed his eyes. Okay. Great. Perfect. "Was the hookup paid for?"

Mel's head reared back as if she'd been struck. "No. I'm not a whore." She shook her head. "That wasn't fair."

Declan leaned forward and swung his empty beer bottle from his fingers. "I'm sorry. Hopefully, you can understand why I questioned it."

Mel nodded. "I slept with you because I liked you. I came back because I liked you. I told him that you owned the bar, which you did. I told him it didn't appear like you or Phil Granger were interested in selling."

"How did you know about Phil?"

"One lunch at the diner and a conversation with Edna." Mel chuckled. "I don't think I could have talked to a more informed individual. Although I suspect she's a little crazy. She thinks UFOs are real."

Declan snorted. "I may or may not have contributed to her belief."

"That sounds like a story I'd like to hear someday." Mel yawned. "Sorry. It's been a long day."

"Yeah. I think we both should get some sleep." Not that he'd be able to, but she looked tired. "You can sleep with me or here on the couch. Your choice."

Mel looked up at him when he stood. "I'm not in the mood for sex."

Declan barked out a laugh. "God, Mel, I never

thought I'd say it, but neither am I. Come on. The bed is more comfortable than the couch."

"I could sleep in the truck. It's not bad."

"No. That's not an option." He held out his hand to her. There was no way he would sleep, but at least he could make sure she was safe. Sleeping in her truck … yeah, that wasn't going to happen again. Not if he could prevent it. Even with his mind churning like a sandstorm tearing up the Gobi Desert, he wouldn't let a pregnant woman sleep in a truck. A pregnant woman who may be carrying his child. That was a line in the sand he wouldn't let her cross.

She took his hand, and they went into the bedroom. He felt out of his element in his own freaking bedroom, which had never happened before. "I have a t-shirt if you want to use it as pajamas." He grabbed one from the drawer and handed it to her.

"Thanks," she murmured and glanced at the bathroom. "I'll be right back."

Declan sat down on the bed and dropped his hands to his head. *Shit.* There was nothing else coming from his muddled brain. He rubbed his face and stood up, stripping beside the bed. He left his boxers on and slid in under the covers.

Mel opened the bedroom door and turned off the light. Declan lay still, waiting for her to get into bed. She padded over and slipped into the far side of the bed. "Thank you."

"For what?" He turned on his side, facing her.

"You could have told me to leave. I wouldn't have blamed you." Mel sounded quiet and defeated. So unlike the woman he'd come to expect. But he didn't really know her outside the bedroom. Hell, they had fun, and he'd liked her, but honestly, he knew practically nothing about her. Well, nothing of substance. How to make her orgasm and scream his name didn't qualify in this situation.

"I'm a lot of things, Mel, but I'm not heartless." He covered her hand with his. "This guy you used to work for. What does he look like?"

"About sixty. Gray hair, a big gut. Balding with a red complexion. Why?"

"No reason." The man at the bar was nothing like the description Mel gave him. A coincidence, maybe.

Mel fell asleep within minutes. Declan stared at the beautiful woman and tried to lasso all his thoughts and bundle them into a problem he could wrangle to the ground. Seemed like there was too little rope and too many problems. He sighed and rolled onto his back, staring at the ceiling. When shit happened in his life, it hit with the force of a Brahma bull spinning out of a chute with a bucking strap cinched tight. Well, he was going to push down his hat and hang on. Only with a baby involved, it wasn't an eight-second ride he was buckling down for … It was a ride that would last a lifetime.

CHAPTER 2

el woke up when Declan got out of bed. Her stomach lurched. She bolted up and rushed past him, sliding to her knees in front of the toilet and grabbing as much of her hair as she could as she heaved. A wet washcloth appeared in front of her after she stopped retching.

"Morning sickness?"

She took the material and held it to her face. The warmth of the water faded quickly, but it was nice to have someone care. Dropping to her butt in front of the toilet, she heard it flush and peeked up from the washcloth. "Sorry."

"I was going to get some coffee. Would you like some?"

"Ah. No. I read caffeine was bad for the baby."

As she moved to push off the floor, Declan was there to help her up.

"Stephanie left some of her frou-frou herbal tea in the cupboards. Would you like some of that?"

"Thank you. I need to go to my truck and get my toothbrush and things."

"I can do that for you. Why don't you grab a shower." Declan headed out of the bathroom. "Towels are clean."

Mel stripped out of Declan's huge t-shirt and started the water. Dropping her panties, she stepped into the stall and shut the frosted glass door. The warm water rained down on her and hid the fact that she was crying. The swell of her belly wasn't huge, but it was noticeable. At least to her.

She'd run the script of what she would say to Declan through her mind a million times. Never had she thought for a moment that he'd be so kind. Declan had a reputation in Hollister. Edna had made sure she knew exactly how much of a womanizer Declan was when she'd visited at lunch with her. But he was also sexy as hell, a charmer, and goodness, the sizzle between them was beyond electrifying. She'd fallen hard and fast. No, she wasn't told to sleep with him. That was something she'd chosen to do. And then she'd chosen to come back. Again and again and again.

Mel wasn't someone who fell on her back for any guy. No, she wasn't easy. She'd had sex a total of four times before she hooked up with Declan. None of those events was life-altering or, hell, even memorable. Declan, on the other hand, she'd remember forever. He coaxed out a devil-may-care attitude and an irreverent sass that she'd always pushed down to be the person her mother cautioned her to be. She could hear her mom's voice. *Be quiet, don't start a conversation with a stranger. Keep your mouth shut, never talk back, and don't sass. No one wants your input. Don't laugh out loud. Your laugh is brash.* But with Declan, she was free, and the times they'd laughed and visited were just as vibrant as when they'd had sex. He'd never told her to stop laughing or suggested she talked too much.

She used his shampoo and lathered her hair. The last time she'd washed it was at a truck stop. She rented one of the showers in the back for a half hour and washed not only herself but her underwear, too. She had a little bit of money. About fifteen hundred dollars. Getting an apartment for her and the baby was the priority. Well, that and a job. And insurance. And a doctor. She leaned against the wall, and the tears started again. Damn it. She wasn't the teary type.

Mel rinsed off and drew a deep breath. She could do this. She would be a great mom. Learning from a bad example of what not to do, Mel knew what to avoid and how not to act. She could do this. Alone if need be. She just needed a break. Or a series of breaks.

By the time she left the shower, her small suitcase was sitting inside the door. She opened it, brushed her teeth, and combed her hair before changing her underwear and putting on her clothes from yesterday.

Declan looked up from the stove as she walked in. "I made some toast, and I'm scrambling eggs. I didn't know what you could stomach."

"Thank you. You didn't have to go to this trouble. I had some protein bars in the truck."

"I saw."

Declan didn't look up from his cooking, but Mel wasn't so sure he wasn't judging her. "I'm doing the best I can," she snapped, then stopped and sighed. "I'm sorry. That was rude and defensive. It's just I don't want people to judge me." She sat down at the table and pushed her wet hair back.

"You mean like I did last night?" Declan put a plate of fluffy scrambled eggs and toast in front of her.

"I deserved it." She waited for him to serve himself and sit down before she picked up a fork.

"Eat a bit of food. Then I have some questions for you." Declan took a bite of his eggs.

She lifted a small portion and carefully ate the first bite. Her stomach stayed where it was supposed to be, so she ate more, finishing the plate and the toast before Declan finished his meal.

"Would you like more?" he asked when she popped the last bit of toast into her mouth.

"No, thank you." She did want more, but she was probably overstaying her welcome as it was.

"Tea?" He held up two boxes.

"Lemon, please?"

Declan put the tea bag in a coffee mug and added hot water. Then he poured a cup of coffee for himself and brought both mugs over to the table. "Ready to talk?"

"Sure." She lifted the bag and watched it sink back down slowly.

"You slept with this other guy once." Declan

was looking at her when her eyes popped up at the statement.

"That's right."

"Why?" Declan put his cup down and stared at her.

She opened her mouth and then shut it because how in the hell did she say it? "It's going to make me seem really petty and shallow."

Declan took another sip of his coffee and lifted his eyebrows, waiting for an answer. "Because I drove out here that second time to see you, but you had your eye on another woman. I was hurt, and he paid attention to me while getting me drunk. Moe kicked us out at closing time. I had sex in his truck with him. I know he wore a condom because I rolled it on him."

"A guy from my bar?"

"Yeah."

"So, I know him."

"I guess." She took a sip of her tea.

"Why did you come back a third time?"

"And a fourth and fifth and sixth time?" Mel quipped. "Because I like you. I told you that." She also liked the sex and the companionship.

There was silence for a long time, and Mel had no idea how to break it. Finally, Declan leaned

25

forward, putting his elbows on the table. "Listen, Mel. I'm not a fan of double standards. We weren't exclusive. I dated, you dated. Just so happens you also got pregnant. I'm willing to do the right thing here."

Mel lifted and leaned forward. "The right thing?"

"Well, as near as I can come to the right thing." Declan ran his hand through his blond hair, making it stand straight up. "I like you. I always have. I'm having a hard time knowing you were sent here to find out shit about me. I don't like that at all." He pinned her with a stare.

"I knew you wouldn't, but I also wasn't going to tell you half the truth." She'd promised herself that. Declan would know the whole truth. She'd never been a fan of lying. Her mom had gotten into a hell of a mess by spinning lies. She wouldn't ever let herself get into that position. At least, she hoped not.

"Okay, this is what I came up with after thinking about it all night." Declan threw a smile at her. "You slept pretty well."

"Yeah, I have to admit the bed was a lot more comfortable than my truck." She stared at him, waiting to hear what he was suggesting.

"I have a six out of seven shot of being that baby's dad. Those are the odds based on the nights we were together, not the number of times we had sex. If you do that math for those odds, since you said you were with the cowboy just once, it's a hell of a lot more likely I'm this kid's dad."

Mel nodded. She'd done the same math. That was why she'd come to tell him he may be the dad. Probably was.

"So, I think we have two options."

Mel cocked her head waiting. *Please, please, please don't say abortion.* She wouldn't do it. Never in a million years.

"One. We can get married."

Mel blinked and then laughed. "No. I'm not marrying someone simply because I'm pregnant."

Declan smiled. "Whew. Dodged a bullet on that one."

Mel grabbed her teabag from the spoon she'd sat it on and tossed it at him. He laughed and grabbed it in the air, placing it on his empty plate.

"What's the second option," she asked.

"I hire you to work at the bar and bring you under my insurance. You stay here with me. We go through the pregnancy together and find out if we're compatible or can't stand each other. At a minimum, we can co-parent knowing each other in ways other than a carnal sense."

Mel glanced down at her nails. "And at a maximum?"

"Mel, I'm not going to declare my love for you. Do I like you? Hell, yeah. Do I want to know for sure if I'm the baby's dad? I do, and we'll figure that out after the baby is born. Will the next five or six months be hard on both of us? Yeah, probably so. But if we have a chance at being good parents, together or apart, I think we need to take it. It stopped being about us when you found out you were pregnant. Even if that baby isn't mine, you'll have a job, a place to stay, and insurance. As to the future, we'll leave that to fate. No expectations, no goals. We'll see where things go."

Mel nodded her head. "And sex?"

Declan blinked and sat back. "Sex is off the table."

Mel frowned. "Why?"

"Because sex could hurt the baby, right?"

Mel laughed at the joke. Only Declan wasn't laughing. She reached out and put her hand on his. "No, sex can't hurt the baby."

Declan shook his head. "Yeah, not too sure I

can be convinced of that. Anyway, do we have an agreement?"

"If the baby isn't yours?"

Declan sighed and shook his head. "We'll cross that bridge when we get to it. Let's just take it one day at a time right now."

Mel nodded. "I can do that."

"Then it's settled. Come in with me to work, and we'll get all the forms filled out. I think it takes time for the insurance to kick in, so we should get that started first." Declan moved over to the coffee pot and poured himself another cup. "Do you want more tea?"

"No, thank you." She hadn't finished what she had. "What are we going to tell people?"

Declan chuckled. "Nothing except that you're pregnant, and I'm the father."

"What? Won't they talk?"

"Oh, hell yeah. But it isn't their business. I figure my sister and Zeke will need to know, but they're closed-lipped with the medical stuff. No one needs to know what's going on. This is between us."

Mel sipped her tea and shook her head. "That could blow up in our faces."

Declan chuckled. "How?"

"I'm not sure. Can't we just say we don't know who the dad is, and you're helping me out?"

Declan shook his head. "No. If we say that, it casts you in a bad light. The people in Hollister might drag you through the mud."

Mel's jaw dropped. "You're willing to have everyone think this baby is yours just so they don't think badly of me?" How could he take that on himself? Why would he? She'd never had anyone stand up like that for her before. The sheen of tears in her eyes made him fuzzy and hard to see.

A moment later, Declan was on his knees in front of her, taking her hands in his. "See, that, right there and the crying in the shower, that's why I'm not going to let people take potshots at you. Yes, I'm going to protect you. I can't let the people who have nothing better to do pick at you. They made Stephanie's life hell, and they chased her away. We let them assume what they want. We don't say anything except you're pregnant and the baby is mine. With you staying here with me, the statement will be logical in their minds. I don't mind saying the kid is mine if it'll protect you. But we don't need to give them anything to feed their insane curiosity while we learn about being parents and being together. If it works out for us, it works out. If it doesn't, we find a way to go forward. But none of that is something we can worry about now. That's a bridge to cross when and if we come to it."

Mel tried, but she couldn't stop the tears. Declan folded her in his arms, and the warmth of his embrace made her cry harder. Of all the scenarios she'd considered, being accepted and protected wasn't one of them.

"Why the tears?" Declan rocked her.

"You … I …" She sniffed and shook her head. How did she tell him that she'd never been given the benefit of the doubt? That no one had ever tried to protect her. She'd only had her mother, and she was an absent adult figure. Melody cried harder. She'd practically raised herself, and no one had ever made her feel safe like Declan. No one made her *feel* like Declan did. He didn't have to do it. He didn't have to care. But he did, and she'd never take that for granted.

CHAPTER 3

*D*eclan walked into the bar area, grabbed the dirty towels, and took them down to the basement to put into the washer while Mel filled out the paperwork for the job and insurance. He read the fine print on the paperwork, and her insurance wouldn't start for six weeks. She needed to see the doctor before that, and he had some money set aside. Not much. The new fire suppression system and roof he'd put in that spring had set him back quite a bit. He filled the soap dish in the washer and put in the towels, hitting the start button.

"Ah, Declan? There's someone here to see you." Mel's voice at the top of the stairs had him taking the steps two at a time. "Who?"

"Me. I believe we met last night. Declan Howard, I presume?"

The stranger was back. He was still wearing clothes that didn't look like he belonged in them.

"I got this, Mel. Thanks." Declan declined the hand presented to him and crossed his arms over his chest. "Who are you, and why are you interested in buying my bar?" The guy was throwing smug vibes around like he owned a case of them and was showing them off.

"I represent an interested buyer."

Declan sighed. Not what he'd asked. "Who are you?" He'd toss the dude if he made him ask again.

"Sean Goins."

"Right, well, Sean, can you tell me why they're interested in the Bit and Spur? This is a tiny town. The revenue from this bar is insignificant for anyone who doesn't live here." Declan turned on his heel and walked up to the front of the bar, leaving the man to follow. He did. Declan wasn't afraid of anyone. He'd been stabbed and punched, had a gun pointed in his face, and he'd blasted a shotgun hole in his roof to stop a fight. He knew people. Working at a bar, you see the best of people and the absolute worst. His gut told him the man was not the mild-mannered businessman he tried to portray. He read more Snake Oil than Fuller Brush.

"They didn't disclose the why, only a dollar amount for the business and the land it's on." Sean walked in front of Declan when he stopped at the hinged door to the bar.

"How much is that?" Declan asked, bored of the conversation already.

"Seven hundred fifty thousand dollars for all the acreage you own here. Cash." The man almost preened when he articulated the cash portion of the offer.

Declan laughed. "No, thank you. I'm not interested in selling. Not for that amount or any other."

"I can bring you another offer," the man immediately countered.

"You do that." Declan laughed. "I'll turn you down, then, too." The man had perseverance. The land the Bit sat on was one hundred acres his pop had bought from Andrew Hollister Senior's father. He had an agreement with Hollister, one he would keep. If he ever sold the land, the Hollister's had the right of first refusal. But he wasn't going to sell. The little bar and the land it sat on was something he could pass on to a child, just like his dad had passed it on to him.

"I wouldn't be so sure." The man knocked on the bar once and turned to leave. That time when he walked out the door, Declan followed him to the door and opened the shutters of one of the windows. He watched the wannabe cowboy get into a big car. Looked like one of those foreign jobs that ran off electricity instead of gas.

"I didn't recognize him," Mel said from behind him.

He turned around at her voice. "Hey. Are you done with the paperwork?"

"I am. Did you know you had about five years' worth of filing stacked in the corner of your office?"

Declan snorted and opened the hinged door to the bar. "Yeah, I do. Do you know I hate anything paperwork related?"

Mel followed him behind the bar. "I could do that for you … if you want. I mean, I'm pretty good at it. I worked in a real estate office before I worked for … well, you know … Mr. Carrington, the guy who sent me here. Anyway, I took care of the front of the office."

"Why did you leave that job?" Declan asked as he lifted three trays of clean beer glasses and moved them over to the middle of the bar where his station was located.

"Ah, well, that would be my mother's doing."

Declan stopped and looked at her. "I never asked. How old are you, Mel?" She'd mentioned her mom several times. Either she had an extremely close relationship with her mom, or her world was really small.

"What? I'm twenty-six. How old are you?" She helped him stack the clean glasses.

"Thirty-four." Declan knew she was over twenty-one. He carded everyone, but because he carded all the new patrons, he never thought about ages past the legal or not legal limit. "Back to your mom?"

"My mom is … well, she's …" Mel sighed and grabbed two more glasses. "She's always got an angle, you know?"

"No, I'm afraid I'm not following."

"Well, for instance, she got me fired from the real estate agency where I worked."

Mel shook her head, and Declan was starting to see why her mother was so prominent in her mind and her conversation lately. Sounded like she was a real witch, but he would wait to pass judgment. "So, what did she do at the real estate agency?"

Mel rolled her eyes but answered him. "She was really interested in the houses going up for sale. I did the flyers between the agencies announcing all the houses, those that were to be staged because they were empty and those that required appointments because they were occupied. My mom visited me one day for lunch and asked me to show her what I was doing. I thought nothing of it. She got the addresses of the houses that were vacant."

Declan stopped working with the glasses. "And?"

"And she gave them to her boyfriend at the time, who stole everything left at the houses … down to the copper tubing used for some of the plumbing. My mom was given probation, swearing she had no idea he would rob the places. I was given the boot, even though I had no idea what she was doing." Mel leaned back against the back of the bar. Her elbows rested on the shelf that held the house liquors. "So, my resume was crap. Being canned for cause isn't a great way to start any interview. I couldn't find a job except for fast food, which paid next to nothing. I had to give up my apartment and move to a friend's apartment and sleep on the couch. I worked slinging burgers while I went for interviews on the side. When I started work for Mr. Carrington, he overlooked my being fired. That should have been my first warning flag."

Declan agreed, but she didn't need to hear that. "Does your mom know where you are?"

"God, no." Mel blurted out. "I love her, despite all her flaws, you know. She's my mom. But at the same time, she's a user. I can't let someone like her be in my baby's life. "I told you I went back home after I found out I was pregnant. I really just needed a place where I could hole up to figure things out. I tried to stay out of sight, but I had morning sickness pretty bad. My mom nagged me until I told her I was pregnant. She was happy to advise me to come back and claim the baby was yours and that I wanted child support. The only part of that advice I took was to come back here. You deserved to know there's a chance this baby is yours. See what I mean about angles?" Mel glanced up at him.

Okay, he was passing judgment. Mel's mom had moved from witch status to straight-up bitch. How had Mel turned out so nice and honest when her mother was obviously the poster image of how not to be a mom? Man, it was completely different from how he and Steph had been raised.

Declan nodded. "Well, you don't have to worry about her now. But, speaking of family, let's head over to Zeke's house. I want to introduce you to my sister Stephanie and her fiancé Zeke, and we need to talk to them about getting an appointment to make sure Junior is doing okay."

Mel drew a deep breath. "Only if you take the cost of the appointment out of my first check."

"I can do that," Declan agreed. He'd never do it, but he agreed.

CHAPTER 4

*M*elody slid out of Declan's truck at a nice house on the edge of town. "This is Zeke and Stephanie's place," Declan said before stepping out and walking around the front of the truck.

He helped her out of her seat, and Mel tugged a bit on his hand when he started to walk toward the door. "Are you sure I should be here? Maybe you should break the news to them by yourself. I mean, I've met Doc Johnson once, but I've never met your sister. It could be awkward."

"Awkward is a family tradition." Declan chuckled and dropped his arm around her shoulder. "We made this baby together, right?"

Mel shook her head. "You don't know that."

"I do. At least until after the baby is born and we do the test. I'm working under the assumption that he or she is mine. We're going to forget about the other guy, and I never want to know who he was."

As they walked to the back door, she asked, "Isn't that a bit like sticking your head into the ground?"

"No, at least not to my way of thinking." Declan knocked on the door.

"You have a strange way of thinking, then." Mel sighed as Declan laughed.

"I do. You should know that by now. Even if most of our time together was spent in bed."

Mel jumped when the door opened, and a blonde woman with a riot of curls answered with a smile. "Declan, what's up?" She looked at Mel, obviously confused but still smiling.

"Hey, Steph. This is Melody. Can we come in, or are you going to make us stand on the porch?"

"Oh, yeah, sure. Come on in. It's nice to meet you, Melody."

"And you," Mel said with a smile in return. Dr. Johnson was sitting on the couch when they came in, but he stood up and shook her hand when Declan introduced her. Declan took a chair across the room from her, and Stephanie sat on the couch, leaving only one chair for her to sit in.

"What's up?" Steph asked.

"Well, I'm going to be a dad."

No one would consider her a shrinking violet, but dang, if she could have melted into the floor, she would have. That was one hell of a bombshell, and Declan's family was in shell shock. Lord, he should have crept up on that explosion instead of detonating it in the front room.

"Excuse me?" Stephanie blinked and looked back and forth between her and Declan.

"I'm pregnant," Mel confirmed what Declan had just said.

"How far along are you, Melody?" Zeke asked.

"As close as I can figure out, almost four months." Mel would have given anything to have Declan hold her hand at that moment, but they were separated by space, on opposite sides of the room. Stephanie and Zeke had the couch, and there was a minefield of emotion between them.

"And you're the dad." Stephanie pointed at Declan.

"Yes." Declan nodded.

"He doesn't know that for sure." Mel wouldn't let him sign up for something he didn't own. Not yet. His family deserved to know the complete truth, too. "I had relations with one other person in the time frame. Only once, and he wore protection, too."

"Too?" Declan's sister parroted. She leaned forward and looked from Melody to Declan, her eyes widening. "Explain that."

Declan sighed and leaned back in his chair. "What do you want me to explain, Steph? I'm always careful."

"Obviously not careful enough." Stephanie mimicked her brother's position.

"No birth control is one hundred percent." Declan shook his head.

Stephanie slapped her legs with open palms. "You're not ready to be a dad, Declan. You're playing the field like a professional baseball player."

"Babe, that's probably *his* decision to make." When Zeke put his hand on Stephanie's, Mel noticed the engagement ring. It was beautiful.

"Thank you." Declan lifted his hands in the air, bringing her attention back to the conversation.

Stephanie rolled her eyes. "I didn't mean to insult you, Declan, but you have to admit, your lifestyle is …"

"My business, but also changing." Declan leaned forward. "Look, I don't owe anyone in this room an explanation of what I'm doing or why except for Melody. But I will tell you this. I've seen this town eat you up and spit you out. I know the hell you went through. If Mel is carrying my baby, I will not allow that to happen. Period."

Stephanie shook her head. "I did a lot of that to myself."

"But not all of it," Zeke interjected. "I can see where Declan's coming from. May I be blunt?"

"Why the hell not? Steph sure doesn't have a problem with it." Declan shot a sharp look at his sister, and Mel hated that the news had obviously placed a wedge between Declan and his sister. How she wished Declan would have broken the news without her. It might've been easier for him. At least, she hoped it would have been.

"What happens if the baby isn't yours?" Zeke leaned back on the couch and pulled Stephanie with him. Mel watched as he put his arm around her and Stephanie glanced at him. The love between them was so evident. That was the type of relationship she wanted one day. Mel looked back at Declan. He was still mad. She could sense it, but he wasn't rude or loud. He glanced at her and gave her a quick smile.

Declan sighed. "Then, as I told Mel, we'll cross that bridge when we come to it. I'm not saying this is a perfect situation. It isn't. But the two of us are going to get to know each other. We're going to focus on the baby and getting along as a couple. If we're never more than what we have been, at least we'll have a foundation for co-parenting."

"*If* the baby is yours, it might not be. She had sex with someone else," Stephanie added. Mel almost physically flinched at the statement. Damn, she couldn't ever see Declan's sister forgiving her for getting pregnant. Maybe Stephanie was being protective of Declan, but it still cut deep.

Declan sighed and stood up. "Steph, do you realize what that sounded like? Jesus, you're being a bitch. Mel doesn't need it, nor do I. I came here to tell you I may be a dad and what our plans are. Thank you for the support."

He walked over and extended his hand to Mel, who took it and stood up. "I'm sorry," she said, not knowing to whom to address the apology, but she felt she had to give one.

"No, I'm the one who needs to say that." Stephanie stood, too, as she spoke. "I'm in a bit of shock, and as much as I hate to admit to Declan being right, he is. That was horrible and bitchy." She walked over to Mel. "I'm sorry. I'd love to get to know you and help in any way possible."

Mel felt herself tear up again. "Thank you. I have no idea why I'm crying. I don't cry." She wiped at her eyes.

"It's called hormones," Zeke said as he stood. "I'd be happy to take you on as a patient, but due to the relationships in the room, perhaps it would be best to ask Eden Wade to see you for your appointments instead."

Declan put his arm over her shoulders and pulled her into his side. The warmth of the embrace made her want to cry again. Damn it, hormones were for the freaking birds. "Thank you, I'd like to know how far along I am and to make sure the baby is okay."

"Are you on prenatal vitamins?" Zeke asked.

Mel froze. She wasn't. Was she hurting the baby by not taking vitamins? "No. Can I buy those at a drugstore?"

"No, they're prescription. I can write you a script, but you'll have to go down to Belle to pick it up. We don't carry them in our mini pharmacy." Zeke dropped his arm over Stephanie's shoulders.

"We can take a run down and pick them up right now," Declan said, and she nodded when he looked at her to confirm.

"Good. I'll call them in while you drive down, and I'll get with Eden on Monday afternoon to set up your visit."

"Thank you." Mel extended her hand to shake Zeke's.

He grabbed her hand in his. "If you have any complications or worries, Declan has our number. Don't hesitate to call. First pregnancies are full of questions, and the only stupid question is the one that isn't asked."

Declan sighed and relaxed next to her. "Thank you. We can see ourselves out."

Leading her to the entry, he opened the door for her, then led her to the passenger side of his truck, where he helped her to find her seat. Mel put on her seatbelt and waited for Declan to get into the truck. "We shouldn't have just dropped it on them like that."

Declan shrugged. "I'm not worried about them. Steph and I are good. Let's head to Belle to get that prescription."

Mel sat quietly as they drove through Hollister and headed south to Belle Fourche. Declan turned on the radio, and she listened to the music while watching the land go by.

"Do you have any allergies?" Declan's question came from nowhere.

"Allergies? No. Why?"

"Just curious. There's a diner in Belle that has good food. I thought we'd eat lunch there." Declan reached over and took her hand in his. "Look, I know this is going to be awkward. I don't want it to be. I want to get to know you. Your likes and dislikes. Where you went to school and what subjects you were interested in. I want to be able to order for you at a restaurant because I know what food you like. I've had one or two girlfriends. Not lately, mind you, but I enjoyed spending time with them. I want that for us."

Mel felt herself tear up again. "When I came to talk to you last night, I never imagined you doing this for me."

Declan squeezed her hand. "I'm doing this for us. For all three of us. I know I have a reputation. Hell, I'm probably known as the town's manwhore, but I'll let you in on a secret." Declan glanced over at her before he looked back at the road. "I'm over the one-nighters."

Mel turned in her seat. "You want a girlfriend?"

"I have for a while. I considered asking you, but you made it clear from the beginning that you were in it for fun." Declan shrugged.

"I said that because I didn't want you to tell me to get lost." Mel shook her head. "I drove back all those weekends because I liked you. You're fun to be with. We laugh at the same things, and I can't deny that you're damn good in bed." Mel chuckled.

"Yeah, I am." Declan straightened behind the wheel and gave her a roguish grin. "But then again, so are you, sweetheart."

Mel rolled her eyes. "I bet you say that to all the girls."

"You're the only girl who's going to hear that from now on." Declan squeezed her hand.

Mel lowered her eyes. "Until the baby is born, and we find out for sure."

Declan shook his head. "Not crossing that bridge until we get to it. Remember?"

Mel nodded. "If you wanted to be with other women, I'd understand." She sure as hell wouldn't like it, but she'd understand. Declan turned to look at her and decelerated quickly, pulling over to the side of the road. "What? What is it?" Mel looked around, trying to see why he'd stopped.

Declan put the truck into Park. "Mel, I don't

know how to make this any clearer. You and I are a couple. Joined by that baby. I'm not going to go after anyone. I'd hoped you'd agree to be exclusive while that baby and our relationship grew. No matter the kind of relationship it ends up being."

Mel closed her eyes for a moment. Declan was too good to be true. "I'd like that. I just didn't want you to feel trapped." She heard her mom's ranting about making the father pony up and pay child support ringing in her ears. She didn't want to trap anyone, which was why she'd told Declan about the other man. The mistake. "I haven't told the other guy. I think I need to."

Declan leaned on the steering wheel and stared down the road as they idled on the side. "I'm not going to lie. I kind of hate that idea." He sighed and turned to look at her.

"I do, too," she agreed. "But shouldn't I tell him?"

Declan turned and took both her hands in his. "Do you know his name?"

"A first name," she admitted, and God, that made her sound like a slut.

"Okay. So, here's my suggestion. If you see him at the bar again, you make the call then. If you don't, well, then finding him would be next to impossible. Right?"

She stared at Declan. He seemed to be pleading with her to agree. "If I see him, I'll have to tell him." It was the right thing to do.

"I'll let you manage that. But until the baby is born and we know for sure he or she isn't ours, then we're exclusive, right?"

"Yes. Absolutely." Mel nodded in agreement. "I never expected this."

Declan laughed and put the truck into gear. "Sweetheart, neither of us did. But we're both in it up to our necks. Time to get comfortable with that fact."

CHAPTER 5

*D*eclan shot an icy glare at the cowboys at the end of the bar. Mel had just served them their beers and headed back into the office to continue meticulously sorting and stacking paperwork into piles before filing it.

"Damn, she's a real looker," one of the cowboys said with a lecherous smirk as he leaned back on his barstool and tried to see where she'd gone. Declan stalked to the end of the bar, dragging his wet rag along the gleaming polished wood as he went.

"Yeah, man. I'd like to have a piece of that," the other agreed with a snicker.

"Not going to happen, boys," Declan said, tossing his bar rag over his shoulder.

"Yeah, why's that?"

"She's pregnant with my kid." Declan planted his feet firmly and glowered at the two assholes as he crossed his arms over his chest.

"Oh, damn. Sorry."

After they muttered their apologies, he walked to the other side of the bar, where Phil Granger sat on his bar stool, staring at him. "Phil. The usual?"

"Yep," Phil said and reached for a bowl of peanuts that Mel had put out earlier. Declan grabbed a frosted glass from the freezer and headed toward the tap. He poured Phil his beer and tossed a paper coaster down on the bar, setting the ice-cold brew in front of the man.

"I assume you heard." Declan stared at his long-time customer.

"I did." Phil lifted his beer. "Congratulations."

Declan smiled. "Thank you."

"You going to marry her?" Phil sat the glass down. "That seems like it would be the right thing to do."

"I know that. We're going to see about that down the road. Right now, we're working things out." Declan set a bowl by Phil for him to discard his empty peanut shells. "Don't figure this is anyone's business but ours."

Phil snorted out a laugh. "Then you've obviously been living in a bubble. Even if I don't say a word, sooner or later, someone in this town will find out, and when they do, everyone will know."

"Prefer that to be later than sooner." Declan winked at Phil before heading down to refresh the beers at the end of the bar.

As he poured more drinks, Mel wandered out of his office with a folder in her hand. "Has this insurance claim been submitted?" She held up the form.

Declan read it and then chuckled. "No. That's from when Zeke broke my window. It's a long story, but I didn't know he'd done it until I'd filled that out. It can be tossed."

"Shredded," Melody corrected him.

"Why shredded?"

"It has personal identification on it. Anything with policy numbers, your driver's license number, things like that need to be shredded." She placed the file on the bar, then showed him another. "What about these?"

Declan leaned over her and looked at the form. He got a lungful of the scent of her shampoo. Lord, he remembered that hair covering him when they had sex.

"Declan?" Mel lifted her eyes to his.

Declan stared at her and smiled. "Sorry. Distracted by memories."

Mel's cheeks turned bright pink. "I was asking if you wanted the invoices filed by date and vendor or just date."

"Whatever you think is best." He ran his hand through her hair.

She smiled up at him. "Date and vendor, then."

"Sounds good." He bent down and gave her a quick kiss. The blush on her cheeks got darker. She picked up the files and scurried back to the office.

Declan turned around to see Phil and Ken Zorn, who'd just entered, staring at him. He shook his head. "The usual, Ken?"

"Ah, yeah … thanks. Is there something you care to share, Dec?"

Ken sat on a bar stool beside Phil as Declan poured the deputy sheriff a diet cola. Phil's snort made him roll his eyes. "About what, man?" Declan played dumb, putting a coaster down in front of Ken.

"Well, besides the obvious, I saw one of those fancy electric cars parked at the bar this weekend. A little too early for a casual stop-by for a beer.

55

Colorado plates, too." After a sip of his soda, Ken grabbed a peanut out of the bowl that Phil was working on.

"Oh, that." Declan sighed. "Let me tell you, that guy was a douche. He came in here late the night before and wanted to talk to the owner. He asked if I knew him." Declan sniggered. "I said I did. He never asked if I was the owner. Idiot."

Both Phil and Ken laughed. "What did he want?"

"Wanted to buy the Bit."

Phil's head popped up, and he held up a hand. "Wait, was this guy wearing new boots and jeans with enough starch to hold him up straight?"

"That would be the guy. Why?"

"He came by the garage and said he had buyers for my garage and land. I told him to take a hike. Gen farms the acreage behind the garage, and we live on the rest. The garage is my only source of income. Why in the hell would I sell? Besides, the Hollister's—"

"Have the first right of refusal. Same. He threw out some pretty numbers, but I told him it wasn't going to happen." Declan took Ken's glass and refilled it with diet cola. "He said he could come back with bigger numbers. I don't know what he expects. The Bit is going to be my kid's inheritance someday."

Ken snorted. "Yeah, that'll be the day. The great love god, Declan Howard, settling down. The earth will shake, and the skies will turn dark. Never going to happen, my man."

Phil Granger choked on a peanut, and Ken reached over and whapped him on the back. "Dude, you okay?"

Phil nodded and cleared his throat. "Yeah, fine."

Ken chuckled and motioned to Declan. "See, man, the thought of you settling down has Phil all choked up, too."

Declan lifted an eyebrow. "Before you start throwing stones, my friend, you should find a woman and settle down. Then maybe I'll listen to your advice." Declan turned away and then spun back. "Nah, never mind. I wouldn't."

Ken smiled ruefully before saying, "You know, if it was up to me, I'd be in a relationship in a heartbeat."

"Yeah, with who?" Phil chuckled. "Let's see … The single women not dating or attached in Hollister are limited. There's Maria."

Declan leaned against the bar and nodded. "Don't forget Dakotah and Brittany."

"Yep, you're right. Then there's Lottie, but she's a bit long in the tooth for Ken here. Oh, Kathy and Kate." Phil snapped his finger and pointed at Ken. "Of course, we can't forget Allison."

Ken cleared his throat and finished his soda. "And before we open that chapter of a book that is closed and permanently affixed to the 'do not open' shelf, I'm out." Ken reached for his wallet like he always did, and like always, Declan declined payment. "You keep coming by. That's all the payment I need. Having that patrol vehicle out front helps legitimize my business for the Sunday morning crowd. As long as the lights aren't flashing."

Ken chuckled. "Ninety-nine percent of that Sunday morning crowd is here at least one Friday or Saturday night a month."

Phil snorted, noting, "Even Father Murphy and Reverend Campbell come by for a cold one now and then."

"A regular social club. I'll catch y'all later." Ken lifted his hand and headed out of the bar.

"You almost choked." Declan rolled his eyes.

"I did choke, but I didn't say a word." Phil eyed his glass. "That's worth a free beer tonight."

Declan put his hands on his hips. "Is this blackmail?"

"I wouldn't necessarily say blackmail … but yeah, pretty much." Phil chuckled, his shoulders moving up and down with his laughter.

"If I give you a free beer, will you keep your mouth shut?" Declan didn't doubt that Phil would call at least three people on the walk home from the bar.

"Oh, yeah, sure." Phil couldn't keep a straight face.

"Get out of here, you old reprobate," Declan growled at him. Phil laughed harder and slid from his stool. "Hey, Phil?" The man turned around. "She's a nice person. I'd take it as a personal favor if, when you spill the beans, you let them know that."

Phil cocked his head and looked at Declan. "You cotton to her, don't you?"

"I do. This isn't a bad thing for me." He was attracted to her, and after learning about her lovely mother, his respect for her had grown. Dealing with that type of crazy couldn't have been easy. The more they were around each other, the more he liked and admired the woman, and there was no question about that.

"I got you. I'll see you tomorrow." Phil lifted his hand and walked out of the bar. Declan served two men from the stockyard and three that came in after work at the meat packing plant. Mel came in and out asking him questions, which he answered. She got a few glances, but the men from the town weren't like the cowboys who had come in earlier.

Zeke and Jeremiah walked in and sat at the bar's far end. "Doctors, what can I get you?"

"Draft, please," Jeremiah said as he reached for a bowl of peanuts.

"Same," Zeke said as he leaned forward to reach under the bar for an empty bowl for the shells.

Declan poured two drafts and set them down before making the rounds and handling refills. When he made it back to Jeremiah and Zeke, Sage had joined them. He'd met Sage about six months ago. The guy was quiet and a semi-regular at the bar. Although he didn't drink, Declan thought he enjoyed the company. Declan pulled a bottle of root beer out of the cooler and popped off the top, putting it in front of Sage on a paper coaster. "How're things?"

Sage took a drink of his soda. "Better." He spoke without stuttering. Declan knew that he was taking treatment for the problem and saw Jeremiah in a professional capacity. Hell, the entire town knew. Just like the entire town would know about Mel being knocked up.

"Eden said she'd see Melody tomorrow at four," Zeke said, taking a sip of his beer.

"We'll close the bar and be there." Declan and Mel had talked about the doctor's appointments. He wanted to go.

"I'll let her know." Jeremiah worked on shelling a peanut. "Congratulations, by the way."

Declan rolled his eyes. So, the word was out. "Thank you."

Sage looked at him and frowned in question at the congratulations remark.

"I'm going to be a dad."

He smiled when Sage's face lit up. "C-congratulations! That's awesome."

"Thank you. Unexpected, but good news just the same. Did Phil call you?" he asked Jeremiah.

"About three seconds after he walked out of this bar." Jeremiah nodded. "He was happier than a pig in slop because he got a free beer out of it. He said to let you know he wasn't telling anyone else, but he had to get a dig in about the free beer. That and he figured I already knew. Which I didn't."

"He's a cagey old fool." Declan had to laugh, though. Phil was good people.

Declan looked up as the door to the Bit opened again and spat out, "Damn it."

Zeke, Sage, and Jeremiah turned to look. "Who's the d-dude?" Sage asked.

"Some guy who wants to buy the bar." Declan flipped his towel over his shoulder. "Excuse me." He walked down to the side of the bar nearest the entrance.

"Back so soon?"

"My buyers are very interested in this lot. They've authorized me to pay one million dollars for the land and the bar."

Declan leaned against the bar and stared at the guy. "Why?"

"I don't ask those questions."

"And I don't see anything in writing."

The man reached into his back pocket, unfolded a sheet of paper, and placed it in front of him. Declan picked it up and read. Once done, he sat the paper down and pushed it with one finger to the go-between. "I'm not a rocket scientist, my friend, but this is not a legal offer. You can tell your people they could offer me ten million dollars, and I wouldn't sell."

"What is so damn fabulous about this piece of shit bar?" The guy grabbed the paper.

"Something someone like you and your bosses would never understand. This bar isn't just my livelihood; it's a central part of the community. We don't have much money around here, but we do have pride, integrity, and a damn good work ethic. You have a shady piece of paper I wouldn't sign if my life depended on it and some mysterious cloud of money backed by anonymous players. I'm not interested. Tell that to your damn backers, and don't come back."

Declan stared the man down, and the guy sighed, "You'll regret not signing this."

"Yeah, the thing is, I won't." Declan turned and walked away from the man.

Mel was behind the bar talking to Zeke, Jeremiah, and Sage, and she looked up when he dropped his arm over her shoulder. "He came back again?"

"Yeah. Like unwanted mold. I told him not to come back. I'm not a real estate savvy person, but the paper he wanted me to sign was written in snake oil." Declan shook his head. "I'll compare notes with Phil in the morning."

"Why does he want the Bit?" Jeremiah asked.

"Not that it isn't a great little watering hole, but it's out in the middle of nowhere."

Mel shook her head. "I don't know, but I do know there's been some interest in the available land around this area."

Jeremiah snorted. "What available land? Don't the Hollisters and Marshalls own just about everything?"

"Minus some of the small ranches that are still making a go of it, yeah. They've never run anyone off, but as people sell, they do buy." Zeke nodded. "That, plus most of the town is owned by the Hollisters."

Declan caught a gesture from one of the men from the stockyard. "I'm not sure what's up, but I put an end to it. I told him not to come back."

Mel put her hand on his arm. "I can take care of them. You visit." She moved to the end of the bar and smiled. Declan shifted so he could see her, making sure no one was inappropriate.

"How much did he offer you?" Zeke took a sip of his beer.

"A million."

Declan dodged a spew of beer. "What?" Zeke sputtered.

Jeremiah handed Zeke several napkins and asked, "Why didn't you take it?"

"First, that document he wanted me to sign was hokey as shit. I smell something really foul with this guy. Why are they willing to pay way more than the land is worth? No, my gut is telling me this is something I need to back away from." He watched as Mel carried a tray of drafts back to the men. His gut told him to back away from the deal, and it told him to grab hold of Mel and the baby. Thankfully, that instinct was rarely wrong.

CHAPTER 6

⚜

*M*elody finished the laundry that Declan had stacked in the laundry room and moved her clothes in with his. He'd cleared half the dresser for her, but she only needed two drawers. Looking around, she took in the moment. Moving her things from the truck into his house was almost surreal. She couldn't have imagined this ending when she'd come to talk to Declan. It seemed Fate had finally smiled on her. She and Declan were getting to know each other, and they were officially living together. "Don't wake up, girl. Don't ever wake up." She rubbed her arms as she stared at the dresser. "He gave up too many drawers." She moved some of his things back to the empty drawers, so they weren't jammed into the other ones.

Declan had gone to the diner to pick up lunches for them, and they'd have to run to Belle or Rapid to stock up on food. She would pay for that. Declan would just have to deal with it. She wasn't there to sponge off him. Mel wandered into the kitchen and made herself another cup of lemon tea. It had become her go-to drink over the last couple of days. With the windows wide open, it was easy to hear the vehicle coming down the drive. Mel went to the front door, expecting to see Declan's truck, but it wasn't.

She put down her cup and went outside as an SUV pulled up beside her truck, and a man got out. He walked over to where she was. "Where is he?"

Mel backed up a bit. The guy in front of her gave off bad vibes. Worse than her mom's boyfriend, who was sent to jail for multiple assaults. "Declan? He's not here. Can I help you?"

The man eyed her up and down. "You live with him?"

Mel crossed her arms over her chest. "How is that your business?"

His hand shot out and grabbed her by the hair.

"It's my business because I choose to make it my business."

Pain shot through her scalp as the man pulled her toward him. "Where is he?"

"I don't know!" Mel gasped in pain as the guy spun her and rammed her into the porch's post. She covered her stomach with her arms, and her face and forehead took the impact. Mel dropped, hitting the concrete stairs when she landed.

"Where *is* he?"

"I don't know!" Mel screamed as he pulled her up by grabbing another fistful of her hair. She saw Declan's truck coming down the drive before she was spun again. She covered her stomach again, anticipating the pain from the next shove. Blinding lights shattered around her. Pain exploded across her cheek, jaw, and neck, and she fell onto the steps, landing hard. She had to get away. She had to protect the baby.

Rolling away from the man, she heard Declan roar, "Mel!"

She got to her hands and knees and crawled toward the house. At the screen door, she looked back. Oh, God! Declan and the man were fighting. Declan was bigger, but the man was fast. He jabbed at Declan and moved in and out quickly. Declan managed to grab the guy from behind as he moved to attack again. Declan lifted him off the ground and threw him to the gravel, going with him as they fell. Declan landed on top of the man and scrambled to his knees, hammering a punch right to the man's face. He did it again.

Mel didn't see the guy move. Declan lifted his fist to hit him again. "Declan, stop." She got to her knees as Declan delivered the punch and raised his fist again as if he hadn't heard her. "Declan, I need help."

His head whipped around, and he was off the guy in a second. "Oh, Jesus." He cupped her face in his hands. "The baby?"

"I covered my stomach." She started to cry now that Declan held her. "He wanted you."

Declan looked back at the unconscious man. "I'm going to get you inside, call Ken Zorn, then get this guy tied up."

Mel nodded and slowly walked into the house. "Couch." She pointed to the soft cushion. He helped her sit down, then ran to the kitchen, returning with a wet towel.

"Are you okay? Are you … is the baby …?" Declan was in front of her, but he looked back out the front door.

"Go. Take care of him." Mel started dabbing at her face. Her tailbone was sore from landing hard on the cement porch, and her face was a tumble of pain.

"Are you sure?"

"Any damage is already done. Get the guy tied up and call whomever you need to call." Mel felt the tears falling and sniffed. "Go."

Declan leaned forward and kissed her gently on the forehead before he got up and raced outside. She heard him slamming around in his truck but couldn't see anything from where she was sitting. And she wasn't going to move.

"Yes, I've got him tied up. What? How the fuck would I know, Ken? He was beating the hell out of Mel when I pulled up. I need to call Zeke. Yes, okay." Declan showed up at the door. He worked the phone as he came to his knees in front of her. "Zeke, I need you out here. Now. Some fucker was beating the hell out of Mel when I got home. What? Yeah, she can. Hold on."

"He wants to talk to you."

Melody took the phone. "I'm here."

"I'm on my way out to you now. Were you struck in the stomach? Are you bleeding vaginally?"

"No, I don't feel like I am. I protected my stomach. My face took the worst of it. I fell hard on the concrete. My tailbone hurts. I hurt."

"Okay. I'm only ten minutes out. If you feel pain or discomfort beyond your face and tailbone, you tell Declan to call me."

"I will." She handed the phone to Declan, then dropped back on the couch.

"They'll both be here soon," Declan said.

Mel nodded. Her mouth, head, face, back, and butt hurt, but she had to tell Declan what had happened. "He pulled up and said where is he? I told him you weren't here. He asked if I was with you or maybe it was if I lived with you." She adjusted to sit on the side of her butt instead of the tailbone, grimacing from the movement. "He grabbed my hair and flung me into the post. Twice. Then you came back." Mel closed her eyes. "Why would he do that? What did he want?" She hadn't had time to be afraid before the man grabbed her. But now, she was shivering from fear. Her entire being ached, and her thoughts centered on her unborn baby. She'd tried to protect the baby. Her arms were bruising a livid purple. Please, please, let her baby be okay.

* * *

As DECLAN DABBED at the scrapes, cuts, and bruises that were getting puffier and darker, he spoke softly and quietly. "I don't know. We're going to find out, though." Her lip was split open, and the side of her face was swelling. "Zeke will be here soon. Everything will be okay." He had no idea if that was the truth or not. He prayed it was. How could that bastard attack a woman like that? He kissed Mel's forehead and wiped away her tears, keeping up the soft comments as he tried to still her fears.

When he pulled up and saw what that fucker was doing to Mel, he'd seen red. Declan wasn't the greatest fist-fighter, but he was a state champion wrestler, and once he got his hands on that motherfucker, he'd put him to the ground. Once there, the bastard was toast, and Declan probably wouldn't have stopped beating him if Melody hadn't said she needed help.

He'd hog-tied that son of a bitch with a rope from his truck. What a fucking waste of sperm. No man worth his salt would lift a hand to a woman. No, that fucker wasn't going anywhere. Declan had made sure his knots were solid and the ropes were tight.

Mel had stopped crying, and he'd cleaned up her wounds as best as possible. He felt useless. He had to do something. "I'm going to grab some ice, okay?"

Mel opened her eyes. "What if he hurt the baby?" That was when he noticed her hands covered her lower stomach.

Declan took one of her hands in his and laid his other hand over hers on her abdomen. "Right now, I'm hoping hard that didn't happen. Zeke will be here soon. I'll get some ice for your lip and the side of your face."

He kissed her temple carefully before he stood up and hustled into the kitchen. He took a tray of ice cubes from the freezer and broke them into a clean towel, then tossed the tray into the sink and wrapped the ice up, twisting the towel to keep it shut. He heard Ken long before the man turned down his drive. The sound of the siren shredded the silence of the country.

He was in front of Mel, holding the ice to the side of her face, when a vehicle pulled up in front of the house. No, it was two vehicles. He heard two doors slam, and a moment later, Zeke was walking into his house. "All right, so what do we have going on here." Zeke put his hand on Declan's shoulder. "Why don't you go help Ken out? I'm sure he's going to want a statement. I'm going to take Mel into your bedroom, and we'll ensure everything is good to go."

"I'm supposed to see Eden this afternoon," Mel said as Declan got up.

"I still want you to go in and see her. We'll just do some of the exam here. Stephanie is calling Eden in now. It isn't a problem. Eden can do an ultrasound at the office. We're just going to make sure nothing happened, okay?" Zeke looked up at him. "I've got this."

Declan nodded and glanced at Mel. "Are you okay with Zeke helping?"

Mel looked up at him. "Yes. I'm okay." There were tears in her eyes, and Declan knew exactly how she felt.

"I'll be right outside," he told her.

He headed out and found Ken sitting on the front bumper of the county's SUV. "You did a good job with the rope." Ken nodded to the man on the ground

"Fucker." Declan spat the word in the man's direction. "He just showed up and started beating on Melody. What the fuck, Ken? What kind of person does that?"

"I couldn't tell you, Declan. But the fucker's name is John Scanlon. Ever heard of him?"

Declan shook his head. "How did you find out his name? Who the hell is he?"

Ken held up an old brown wallet. "Well, according to the NCIC check I ran, he's a felon out of New York. He's wanted for several counts of assault and extortion back in New York, at least according to dispatch."

"New York?" Declan rubbed the back of his neck. "What in the hell is some New York criminal doing in my front yard?" The day went from nice to shit in two point three seconds, and now, it was getting all kinds of weird.

"Do you have any enemies in New York?" The question was probably meant to be a joke, but Declan wasn't in the ha-ha mood.

"Ken, you know I've never gone farther east than Sioux Falls. What in the hell did this guy want?"

"That's what we'll find out when he comes around. Zeke did a quick pulse check on him before he went into the house. How's she doing?"

"I don't know, man. I saw him fling her into

that post by the hair. That son of a bitch!" Declan yelled. He needed to hit something.

"If what he did makes her lose the baby, he's going to jail for a long, long time." Ken spit toward the man on the gravel. "Congratulations, by the way."

Declan plopped his ass on the bumper, sitting down with Ken. "Thanks." The fire in his gut still burned white hot. The bastard had thrown her into the post. Thrown her. Declan shook his head. "Man, the shit that went through my head when I saw him throwing Mel. I don't think I've ever been this mad before in my life."

"Not even at Andrew?" Ken chuckled.

"That was a slow boil, and I was madder at the town than Andrew. He was just a target for my unsolved angst."

"Shit, you sound like Doc Wheeler."

Declan huffed. That was because he'd talked to the Doc about his feelings toward Andrew Hollister. Declan shook his head. "That's all water under the bridge, but no. This is different. Mel and the baby are my responsibility." Declan dropped his elbows to his knees. "Damn it, if he hurt that baby, you won't have to put him in jail."

Ken didn't say anything for a moment. "I'm

going to need a statement from Mel. I know you don't want to hear this, but maybe this guy came out here because of her, not you."

Declan turned his head slowly to look at Ken. "Explain that."

"Well, what do you know about her past? Look, I'm not saying anything bad about her, but it's a line of questioning I'll have to pursue."

"You do what you have to do. I don't care why he was here. I want him gone."

"I know. I've got a tow truck coming to get his car. I want the big boys with all the pretty toys to go through that thing. He's under arrest. He just doesn't know it yet. But he's a career criminal. If he has half a brain, I'm not going to get any information out of him. He's going to opt for a lawyer. It would be different if I weren't an officer of the law. A little incentive might make him flap his jaws. Of course, I couldn't use any information gained that way against him. But it might be nice to know what he does. If you know what I mean."

Declan turned to look at his friend. "I believe I understand." Ken would give him a go at the asshole to find out information.

"Understand what? You must've been dreaming, Declan. I've just been sitting here enjoying the sunshine, not saying anything."

"Yep, I guess I was," Declan agreed with Ken.

The man they were talking about jerked, his eyes opening wide. "Well, there you are." Ken stood up and walked over to the man. He bent down and pushed his cowboy hat back on his head. "Now, I'm not sure how they do things way out there in New York City, but we don't beat up on no woman around here. Especially a pregnant woman. That could get you lynched in these parts. It's a lucky thing I happened to be in the area. But because you did rough up that little lady, I'm placing you under arrest. You have those Miranda rights. I'm sure you know the ones I'm talking about. The right against self-incrimination and to have a lawyer present when we question you because we will. I'll read them to you later in case getting your bell rang made you a little loopy."

"Fuck you. I want a lawyer," the man growled back.

"Ah, see, that's not neighborly, friend." Ken stood up, pulled out his cuffs, and put them on the bastard. "You got a knife?" He grinned at Declan. "Maybe you can cut these ropes off while I go in and see if I have additional charges to make against this man."

"Gladly." Declan stood up and moved into view of the man on the ground. He leaned down and smiled. "I hope I don't miss, you know, with that rope running between his legs like it is."

Ken chuckled. "I'm sure you'll do what's right. I mean, he did beat up the woman carrying your baby." Ken turned and walked to the house.

Declan grabbed his hunting knife from his truck and made a show of drawing it out of the sheath in front of Mr. New York. "Why are you looking for me?"

"Fuck you," the man spat toward Declan.

"No, thank you. You aren't pretty enough." Declan grabbed the rope that ran from the man's hands to his feet and pulled it up in the air. The guy's balls were under that rope, and the high-pitched whine that came out of the stranger would have been funny under any other circumstances. "Why did you come out here looking for me." Declan pulled the rope harder, and Mr. New York yelped. "Not an answer."

He tugged with a couple of sharp pulls. The man gasped, "Paid."

"Ah, see, that wasn't so hard. Who paid you?"

The guy growled, and Declan jerked the rope again. His balls had to be sore by then. "Don't know. Got the money and instructions. No names."

"What were you supposed to do?"

The man growled but didn't answer.

"Fuck—" Mr. New York's scream when Declan yanked on the rope brought Ken out of the house. "Everything all right out here?"

"Sure, sure … the knife is kind of dull, and I had to yank the rope a couple of times. No problems." Declan didn't look at Ken, but he smiled at the fucker whose balls were probably the size of cantaloupes about then.

"What were you supposed to do?" Declan asked when Ken went back into the house.

"Fuck you."

Declan cut the rope, and the man dropped to the ground. "I told you, you're not pretty enough." Declan pulled the guy's hair, lifting him. "You hurt the mother of my baby. If that baby is injured, you won't need to worry about how swollen your balls are. I'll cut them off and feed them to you. Out here in the wild, wild west, we know how to castrate, and we don't use anesthesia." Declan dropped the guy's head, and his face planted in the gravel. Declan headed toward the house.

Ken met him on the porch. "What did you find out."

"Not much. According to him, he was paid to come out here. He said he didn't know who had paid him. He said he'd just received instructions. He wouldn't tell me what he was supposed to accomplish with all this shit." Declan glared at the fucker who was handcuffed on the ground. "I could work on him some more."

"Nah, you probably got as much out of him as he was willing to divulge. Once the tow truck gets here, I'll take him and his car south. I'll be back later tonight and stop by to get a statement from Melody and you, too." Ken clasped him on the shoulder. "If she has complications, you let me know."

"Zeke didn't say?"

"They're still in the bedroom. I wasn't going to interrupt."

Declan nodded and glanced up at the sky. "Do you think this could have anything to do with the people wanting to purchase my land?"

Ken crossed his arms and drew a deep breath.

"It crossed my mind. There are a lot of unanswered questions."

Zeke came to the screen door. "Declan, can I see you for a minute?"

Ken clasped Declan on the shoulder. "I'm here until I get the tow truck settled. You take care of business."

Declan nodded and headed into the house.

"Are they okay?"

"Yeah, I think so. He did a number on her face, but nothing was broken. There's extensive bruising on her arms where she blocked herself from running into the post with her abdomen. A mother's instinct is a real thing. Never let anyone tell you it isn't. We'll know more when Eden does an ultrasound, but I'm fairly confident she dodged a bullet. I've arranged for Eden to come in early. Mel's waiting for you. I'll follow you into the office. Has anyone told you that you have one hell of a shiner?"

Declan blinked. "No. Do I?" He lifted his hand to his face.

Zeke huffed, "You do. Other eye."

He'd taken a couple of punches, but he was fine. He couldn't feel any damage.

Zeke leaned forward, stared into his eyes, then

leaned back. "Keep your head still and follow my finger. He lifted his finger and moved it. Declan followed the movement. "Looks okay, but I'll take a better look at it at the office."

"Thanks for everything, man." Declan headed into the house to get Melody.

CHAPTER 7

*D*eclan insisted on carrying Mel into the clinic, and she didn't argue. Her butt hurt. God, it really hurt, and sitting on her tailbone was painful to the extreme. Walking was better, but any movement, like getting in or out of a chair, hurt.

Zeke opened the door and pointed to an exam room. "We're waiting for her in there."

Declan carefully weaved through the door and gently placed her on the exam table. She winced and rolled to alleviate the pressure on her tailbone.

"Hi. Melody, right? I'm Eden Wheeler," a blonde woman said as she entered the room. "I'm going to do your exam today and find out what's going on with you and the kiddo. Okay?"

Mel nodded her head. "Please." She was terrified, even after being reassured by Dr. Johnson.

"Gentlemen, if we can have the room?" Eden spun and looked at Dr. Johnson and Declan.

"Can't I stay?" Declan's hand covered hers.

Eden smiled. "Well, I'm going to do a pelvic exam first. After that, I'm going to do an ultrasound. I'll call you in for that. Deal?"

Declan looked down at Mel. "Is that what you want?"

She nodded. "I'll be okay."

"Come on, slugger," Zeke said. "We'll grab a cup of coffee with Stephanie. She's been worried about you and Mel. I made her stay in the office, but she's going to bust through that door if she doesn't get eyes on you soon."

Declan cast one more glance in Mel's direction, and she nodded. "Go see your sister."

Eden shut the door after the men were through it. "So, have you had an exam since you found out you were pregnant?"

"No. I don't have insurance. Well, not yet. Declan hired me, and the insurance will start in a month or so." Mel leaned to her side and winced.

"What's going on here?" Eden motioned to the lean.

Mel shook her head. "I fell on the porch. I think I landed against one of the cement steps. It hurts to sit down."

"Any abdominal discomfort?" Eden held onto her arm. "Let's get you down and into a gown."

"No, I don't think so. I mean, my hips hurt, but I think it is more of a tailbone discomfort." Mel tried to straighten. "I've gotten bucked off a horse and landed on my tailbone when I was growing up. It feels like that."

"Ah, okay. First, I would recommend no horseback riding. I can get an x-ray of your tailbone, but it isn't something I'd want to do because of your pregnancy. And honestly, even if it's broken, when you're pregnant, the outcome from a medical perspective is the same unless you have severe pain when using the bathroom. If you do, I need to know. I'll do an exam after we do the pelvic exam to see if there's too little or too much motion of the coccyx. If everything is normal, I'll give you a coccygeal cushion, or a foam donut, for you to sit on. Kegel exercises can help to strengthen the pelvic floor, which will help. You know about those?"

Mel nodded. "I do."

Eden nodded. "If you sleep on your back, sleep

with a pillow under your knees. On your side, a pillow between your knees. No sex until you're comfortable."

"Sex won't be a problem. Declan thinks having sex while I'm pregnant will hurt the baby."

Eden laughed and shook her head. "Men. Bless their hearts. They're so misinformed."

"Yeah, I tried to tell him." Mel leaned forward instead of trying to straighten up.

"Let me get a gown for you to change into. I'll help you back on the table." Eden went to a cabinet and came back with a pink gown. "It ties in the front." She continued, "I'll turn my back and get some medical history from you as you change. When you're ready, let me know, and we'll get this show on the road."

Mel pulled off her t-shirt and put her hand over her abdomen, saying a silent plea to the heavens that her baby was okay.

* * *

DECLAN ENDURED the hug from Stephanie. "What happened."

Declan glanced at Zeke. "Didn't you tell her

what happened?" He was pretty sure Zeke would have spilled everything already.

"I did." Zeke shrugged. "She wants to hear it from you."

"From the horse's mouth, Declan." Stephanie poked his stomach.

"Ouch, damn it, Steph, I don't need you beating me up." That finger of hers was freaking dangerous. Declan swatted her hand away as she came at him again.

"I went to the diner to get us lunch to-go. We've got to go south and do a big grocery run. There was nothing in the fridge or cupboard that either one of us wanted." He shrugged. It happened. "When I came back, I saw another truck in front of the house. As I got closer, I saw this fucker swinging Mel by the hair into the square wooden post at the stairs of the porch. I got into it with him. I took a couple of punches before I was able to grapple him to the ground."

Stephanie's eyebrows lifted. "Your eye is a beautiful shade of black and blue. Is he still alive?"

"Yeah," Declan snarled. "He hurt Mel. If he hurt our baby, being behind bars is the only thing that will save him."

Steph smiled at him. "Our baby."

Declan narrowed his eyes at his sister. "Do not start with me." He was a mess right now, and he wouldn't deny it was screwing with his head. The fear and anger had faded, but he was worried. And there was a multitude to be concerned about. The baby's health, Mel's health … what that asshole did and why. But most of all, the resounding truth that he wanted that baby. He needed both the baby and Mel to be okay, and he wouldn't take any shit from anyone about that fact. They could think what they liked, but he was certain he was all in with Mel and the baby. Which was why he was going insane. He'd classify himself as Def Con One in the worry department.

Steph shook her head. "I wasn't being a witch. I promise. I think you'll make an awesome dad. I just wish you would've had the choice of when to become one." The bell at the front door jingled. "I'll get that." She toed up and kissed him on the cheek. "Eden and Zeke will do everything they can."

Zeke handed Declan a cup of coffee. "Not the shot of whiskey you probably need right now, but it'll have to do."

"Thanks." Declan dropped into Stephanie's chair, suddenly exhausted. "Man, I can't get the sight of her slamming into that post out of my mind." It replayed like a boomerang video. Over and over without stopping.

"I get it." Zeke sat down in the only other chair in the office. "You like this girl, don't you?"

Declan huffed and ran his hand through his hair. Man, people's opinion of him must really suck. "Why does everyone seem to think that's an impossibility?"

Zeke chuckled. "Asks the man who takes a different woman home almost every weekend."

Declan shook his head and stared at the steam coming off his coffee. "Not lately, man. I've slowed way down. It was just sex. Most of it wasn't good. I like her, yeah. I considered asking Mel to start dating instead of hooking up, but she said she wasn't interested in a relationship, and then she fell out of sight." He took a sip of his coffee. "Of course, she admitted she said that because she didn't want me to dump her."

"Would you have?" Zeke lifted his legs and propped them on the corner of Stephanie's desk.

Declan sighed. Would he have? God, he didn't know. If she'd come out and told him she liked him … there was a fifty-fifty shot, depending on the day. "I couldn't tell you. I have no idea what I would've done, but I know what I'm doing *now*."

Declan glanced over at his soon-to-be brother-in-law. "I want to hold her close and keep everything that can hurt her away. Jesus, Zeke, I've failed at that, and we've been together for less than two weeks."

Zeke nodded. "You haven't failed, Declan. You didn't know this guy would show up. None of us did. This was a freak thing. There's no way this is on you." He glanced at the door and then looked back at Declan. "Sex isn't a bad way to start a relationship, but it can't be the only thing you base it on."

Declan snorted. "Zeke, she's pregnant. What sex are you talking about?"

Zeke dropped his feet and leaned forward. "I'm not following. What are you talking about?"

"We *can't* have sex. She's *pregnant*." Declan shook his head. "I don't want to hurt the baby."

Zeke smiled and then chuckled. "Ah, Declan, you can't hurt the baby by having sex. Nature has provided a warm, comfortable bubble for your kid. He or she won't be disturbed by you having sex with Melody."

Declan stared at Zeke and narrowed his eyes. "No shit?"

"No shit, just don't go crazy, no kink or whips

and chains," Zeke answered and started laughing. Full-on belly laughs.

Declan rolled his eyes. "Dude, stop laughing at me before I get a complex."

"What are we getting a complex about?" Stephanie said as she came into her office.

Declan stood up to give her the office chair. "Whips and chains."

"What?" Stephanie's face screwed up. "What are you talking about?"

"Nothing, you kind of had to be here. Who was out front?" Zeke wiped his eyes as he asked. The bastard. Well, at least he didn't spill the beans to Stephanie. Declan hoped he'd keep that between them.

"Two guesses and the first two don't count," Stephanie said as she sat down.

"Edna Michaelson," Zeke guessed.

"Bingo. She saw Declan carrying some poor woman into the clinic and had to come to see if there was anything she could do because she'd heard that Declan was going to be a daddy, and if that was the woman who was pregnant, well, then, she wanted to see if she could help out in some way."

Declan sighed. "That woman." He was on the

fence about Edna being a run-of-the-mill busy-body or an evil minion who spread rumors and fanned the hell-fire flames of gossip.

"Don't worry. I managed to get her out of the building without saying a word. I'm getting really good at managing her nosiness. Of course, I watched her go straight back to the diner. I don't know how Gen, Ciera, and Corrie deal with that bunch of hens."

"They ignore them, just like you should." Zeke smiled at her. "I know your feelings about gossip, but those ladies aren't vicious. They're just curious."

Declan leaned against the door and tuned out the rest of the conversation. His eyes were glued to the exam room door. He wanted to be in there with Mel.

When the door finally opened, Declan almost sprinted to it. "Is she okay? And the baby?"

"Settle down, Dad." Eden chuckled. "Come on in. We're ready to do the ultrasound."

He strode straight to the exam table. Mel wore a hospital gown and had her knees propped up by a pillow. "Are you okay?" Declan bent down and kissed her forehead.

"I am." Mel nodded.

"All right. This will be cold. Sorry." Eden split open the gown and applied some type of clear goop to Mel's lower abdomen. Declan realized there was a small bump he hadn't noticed before. He'd given her privacy because he was sure they couldn't have sex, and seeing her naked would jolt his lust into hyperdrive. But he could see a definite swell to her once flat stomach. That was his baby. *His baby.* Holy fuck. His knees almost buckled.

"Whoa there, big guy. If you go down, I won't be able to catch you." Eden grabbed a chair and put it right behind him.

"That's our baby," he whispered to Mel as he plopped his ass in the chair.

She had tears in her eyes when she turned to him. "It is."

Eden chuckled. "If you're shocked about that, wait until you see this." She pointed at the screen. Declan fixated on the little monitor as Eden moved some type of device over Mel's stomach. "There. There you go." Eden pointed to the middle of the screen. "That's your baby. From the information Mel gave me, I think she's between thirteen and fifteen weeks pregnant. We should be able to determine the sex if this little one will cooperate."

Eden moved the wand and then cocked her head. "Huh."

Declan snapped his head in her direction. "What? What's wrong?"

Eden shook her head. "Nothing. Just let me adjust this." She manipulated the ultrasound wand thingy again and then looked at Mel and Declan. "Well, it appears we have a bit of a surprise."

"What?" Mel gripped his hand and damn near crushed it.

"Look here. This is a nub, which based on the angle, means this little guy is a boy."

"A boy!" Declan kissed Mel's hand. "We're going to have a boy."

Eden smiled wide. "And this, this little nub, is also a boy."

Declan blinked and snapped his head to Mel, whose eyes were as wide as saucers. "We're having twins?" they asked at the same time.

Eden nodded. "Twin boys, and everything looks great. Placenta and gestational sacs look good. Let me do a measurement, and we'll be able to know with more certainty how far along you are." Eden manipulated the machine and then turned something on. A fast, whooshing sound came out of the speaker. "Heartbeat for baby number one." She moved the gadget in her hand around, and the whooshing filled the room again. "Heartbeat for baby number two."

Overwhelmed, he held onto Mel's hand. Twins. They were going to have *twins*.

CHAPTER 8

Mel sat on her foam donut, her legs up on the couch with pillows under her knees. Declan had been crazy all afternoon. She watched him pace from one room to the next. "What are you doing?"

"I'm going to have to put an addition on the house." He ran his hands through his hair. "I don't have enough time, though. I could go through that wall," he said, pointing to one side.

He went back into the bedroom and came out. "Or we can move into the old place. Steph cleaned it up when she was using it. It needs a lot of work still, but I think that's the more viable answer. It needs a new furnace. I haven't fixed it. I need to buy a furnace. And get someone to install it. I'm crap with electricity. Shit, I don't know if I have to make more room for the furnace over there."

"Declan." She called to him as he went into the kitchen.

He was back in the living room in a second. "Do you need something?"

"Yes, for you to sit down and talk to me." He sat on the floor beside her. "Thank you. First, the babies don't need a room for themselves right away. Second, if they aren't yours …"

Declan's head snapped up. "Mel, I know I can be a bull in a China shop sometimes—"

"Sometimes?" Mel lifted an eyebrow.

Declan laughed. "Okay, but you knew that about me when we were just hooking up. Don't try to deny it."

"I wouldn't." She laughed with him.

He smiled at her. "The sex between us is amazing. I like you, and you like me. I want to make this work."

She put her hand on his cheek. "Declan, wanting to make it work and forcing the issue are two different things." She delicately ran her finger over the bluish-purple slash under his eye. "We take things one day at a time. That's what we agreed on. If, and I stress *if,* in the future, an addition to the house is needed, then we cross that bridge when we get to it. Right?"

He sighed and leaned into her touch. "Right."

Mel turned to look at the front door at the same time as Declan because of the sound of gravel crunching under tires. He was up and holding the rifle he now kept by the door a moment later.

"What?"

"Who is it?"

"Looks like the whole town. Hold on." He stepped out of the house, the gun still in his hand.

Mel twisted to try to see out the screen door. She heard several voices before Declan came back into the house. "Who is it?" Mel asked.

"I was wrong. It's just half the town," Declan said, opening the door.

Stephanie led the way with two bags of groceries. "Hey, Declan mentioned you needed to stock up on groceries." She headed into the kitchen.

"Hi, Melody, I don't think we've met. I'm Gen Hollister. I own the café in town. I brought some frozen meals and some food for tonight."

Melody's mouth dropped. "Thank you so much."

Gen smiled broadly. "No problem whatsoever.

My husband is bringing in some fresh veggies and fruit from our garden." She marched into the kitchen with Stephanie, and they started laughing. A tall cowboy with dark hair and the bluest eyes she'd ever seen walked in after her. He nodded his head. "Ma'am."

Melody lifted a hand and waved because she had no idea what else to do.

"Hey, Melody." Eden Wheeler came in with a huge box. "This is my husband, Jeremiah. You've probably met him before. But I have all these maternity clothes that I won't be using again. I know the pants might not work, but you can cut them off into shorts. The tops should fit you, and I have about ten dresses the size of tents in here, too."

Mel struggled to sit upright. "That's so sweet! Thank you." She winced as she sat wrong on her tender derriere.

"Don't move. We'll be out of your hair in just a minute." Eden put the boxes down beside the couch. "Has the idea of two boys sunk in yet?"

"Not even in the slightest. I think Declan is going to have a nervous breakdown. He wants to put an addition on the house. Tonight."

Eden laughed and shook her head. "He'll make

a good dad. Thank goodness you're not having girls. They tend to be overprotective."

"I resemble that remark." Eden's husband, Jeremiah, winked at Mel. "I'm going to go hang out with the guys until you get done. Nice seeing you again, Mel."

"Nice seeing you, too," Mel said as he and Gen's husband left. "This is so sweet. None of you had to do this."

Stephanie and Gen came into the living room from the kitchen. "We didn't have to, but we wanted to." Steph sat down across from Melody. "I was a bitch when Declan brought you over. I hate that I was, and I'm so sorry. I'd love to be friends, and Gen and Eden are two of my best friends in town. We got together after you left and decided we needed to be the Hollister welcome wagon. You know, before Edna figures out you're living out here and develops a reason to stop by."

Mel chuckled. "I've had lunch with Edna. She's … unique."

Gen laughed. "That's the truth. But she's harmless, for the most part."

Eden put her hand on Stephanie's shoulder. "I need to get home."

Steph laughed. "That was my cue for not

staying too long because you've had a very stressful day. We had it prearranged because I'm …"

"Talkative?" Gen suggested.

Eden fanned a hand over her chest, "I'll have you know that cue was nicely delivered."

Gen laughed. "We'll get out of your hair for now. But expect visits."

"Thank you all so much."

Stephanie bent down and hugged Melody. "Congratulations. I'll pop in tomorrow to check on you at lunchtime."

"I'll be fine. Declan said he would have Moe open the bar tonight and tomorrow."

Stephanie lifted an eyebrow. "And you're sure you won't need a break from him?"

Melody laughed. "I'm sure. But if you want to stop by, please do."

"Believe me. She will," Declan said from the door. "Zeke said to tell you to shake it. You promised to make him pumpkin pie."

Stephanie stood upright. "That's right, I did. I'll see you tomorrow." She jogged out of the house before Mel could say goodbye.

"They're so nice." Mel reached for the box Eden had placed next to her and lifted a beautiful top.

The generosity was beyond anything she'd ever experienced.

"Well, with the fun also comes the pain." Declan stood looking out the door.

"What? What's wrong?"

"Nothing. Ken Zorn is pulling up the drive. We're going to have to give our statements about what happened today, and he's going to ask questions."

"About?"

"I don't know, but he always asks questions. I think it's in his nature. Makes him a good cop." Declan glanced into the kitchen. "Do you want some tea? Stephanie brought some more."

"Lemon?"

Declan smiled. "Lemon it is. I'll put the water on to heat as soon as Ken comes in."

* * *

DECLAN MET Ken on the porch. "How's she feeling? I stopped by the Bit and saw Moe was opening, so I came here."

"I'm doing much better. Thank you," Mel called from the front room.

Declan chuckled and opened the screen door.

Ken took off his cowboy hat and walked in. "Melody. We've never really met, but I've seen you a time or two in the bar here lately. I'm Ken Zorn, the deputy sheriff in these parts."

"Hi, Ken," she greeted and pointed to the chair Stephanie was sitting in. "Forgive me for not getting up."

"No worries. Do you feel well enough to give me your statement?"

"I do, although there's not much to tell."

Declan asked from the front door, "Ken, something to drink?"

"Water?"

"You got it." Declan went into the kitchen while Melody told Ken about her brief encounter with the bastard who beat her up. He put the water on the burner for tea and got Ken a glass of ice water.

"So, he said, 'Where is he'?" Ken asked again. "Thank you." He took the glass of iced water from Declan but didn't drink it, waiting for an answer from Melody.

Declan sat down on the floor beside her. "Yes. My response was, 'Declan? He's not here.'"

"The attacker didn't say Declan's name?"

She shook her head. "No."

Ken nodded. "I have to cover all the bases on

this case, so forgive me for asking, but is there anyone in your past who would have a grudge against you? Anyone who might be angry with Declan for being the father of your baby?"

Melody's jaw dropped, and she shook her head. "No. Absolutely not."

"Are you sure?" Ken took a drink of the water.

"I don't have any estranged boyfriends or lovers. I have no one in my past who would send a man to hurt Declan or me." Melody shook her head. "Of that, I'm positive."

"Why are you asking, Ken?" Declan took Mel's hand in his.

"The investigators down south dug further than I can. This guy has connections in Colorado. Mel's from that area. It was a loop I needed to close."

"That's understandable." Mel nodded. "He just grabbed my hair and flung me into the post. It all happened so fast."

Ken nodded and opened the file he'd brought in with him. "This is a series of pictures. Would you please pick out the man who attacked you?"

And that hit a bump in Declan's brain. "Why? You know who did it. Why are you having Mel pick the guy out of a lineup?"

"Right, but Mel didn't identify him to me as her attacker. I need confirmation."

"He attacked me." Declan pointed to his face. "I can confirm he's the one who attacked her."

"Which you will do in your statement." Ken sighed. "Declan, I'm not trying to be argumentative or anything here, but I'm doing my best to make sure there's no wiggle room and this bastard doesn't get away with what he's done."

Mel squeezed his hand. "I remember vividly what he looked like. I'll be happy to pick him out."

Declan leaned over and took the pictures from Ken. He handed them to Mel and watched as she went through the six pictures. The men all looked close to what the attacker looked like. Mel lifted the attacker's picture. "This is the man who threw me into the porch post. Twice. He also lifted me by my hair, and I fell against the cement steps, which caused an injury … to my tailbone." She handed the pictures back to him, and Declan passed them to Ken. Scumbag's photo was on top.

"Thanks, Mel. Do you think you could write all that down for me? I have a form here."

"Sure." She took the paper and pen attached to a clipboard from Ken.

"Start with the date and approximate time if

you could," Ken said as the kettle in the kitchen began to whistle.

"I'll get your tea." Declan stood up and headed into the kitchen. Ken joined him before he'd finished pouring the hot water on the teabag.

"Moe said to tell you someone came by to talk to you before the bar opened. Name of Sean Goins. He told the guy you were out from work for a while." Ken leaned against the bar.

Declan snapped his head to look at Ken. "That's the one who wanted to buy my place."

Ken nodded. "Could be a coincidence."

Declan leaned against the counter and stared at the teabag. "Doesn't seem like a coincidence to me."

"Me, either. I'm going to run the name and get with the sheriff to get him to authorize me to start a case lateral to the one the guys down south are running against our attacker. Something stinks."

"To high heaven," Declan agreed. "Do you need a statement from me?"

"Yep. I only have one clipboard, so you can do yours when Melody is done. Hey, I hear you're having twins. Congratulations."

Declan shook his head. "Dude, news in this town …"

"Travels like the wind." Ken chuckled. "Phil Granger told me when I was at the bar. He said Edna overheard Gen and Ciera talking about it in the kitchen at the diner."

"Lord, that woman." Declan dropped his head back between his shoulders and stared at the ceiling.

"Your fault." Ken chuckled.

"Say what?"

"Dude, you're the one who invited her to the Bit with those cronies of hers. She's adopted you into her inner sanctum. I think she's a little bit in love with you."

Declan contorted his face. "Man, she's in her sixties!"

"Closer to seventies, and the heart wants what the heart wants." Ken laughed and jogged out of Declan's reach, his gun belt and keys jingling as he went into the living room.

"With friends like you, I don't need enemies." Declan picked up Melody's tea. But he was damn lucky to have friends like Ken. Damn lucky.

CHAPTER 9

Melody carried her donut into the Bit and Spur. Declan had steadfastly refused to let her come to the bar for the last week. But Stephanie, Gen, Eden, and their friends Allison and Kathy had all checked in on her. Declan had been so attentive. He'd made up a silly routine during dinner. They swapped one detail of their lives before they'd met. Only it was never just one detail. She'd laughed so hard she'd cried. Declan must have been a handful growing up. Telling him about her life wasn't as much fun, but she managed. When she was living it, it was all she knew. As she grew and started to escape her mother's influence, she realized she'd been used, and that was abusive. Declan was attentive and listened. He never criticized her decisions or her mother. And that was … oddly comforting. She loved her mom, but she couldn't let her back into her life. Even with the wonderful dinner conversations, she was glad to be back at work. Having a purpose was energizing. She wanted to help Declan as much as he'd been helping her, and Declan's office needed a lot of help. Today was Friday, so the bar would be hopping.

Declan opened the office door. "If I need help out front, I'll let you know."

Mel turned and put her hands on her hips. Her jeans were too tight, and she'd left the top fastener undone, but that was hidden by one of Eden's maternity shirts. "Are you trying to keep me away from the bar?"

"Yes, yes, I am." Declan crossed his arms over his chest. "You don't need to be out there. What if some drunk lights up a cigarette?"

"You'll do what you always do, make him put it out or kick him out. Honestly, Declan, I'm pregnant. You don't need to wrap me in bubble wrap."

She watched it happen. A smile kicked up at the corner of his mouth and then spread across his face. He reached down and took her donut, lifting it between them. "Oh, really?"

Mel groaned, but she had to laugh, too. Dear God, the man was irresistible. "Okay, you can bubble wrap my ass."

Declan tossed the donut onto his desk and wrapped his arms around her. "That would be awkward, and it would make sex difficult, too."

"Sex?" Melody let her hands slide up his big, muscled arms. A shiver went through her.

"I have it on good authority that the boys are pretty well protected."

Mel lifted her eyebrows. "You listened to me?"

Declan wagged his head. "Yes and no. I may have mentioned to Zeke that I couldn't have sex with you because you were pregnant. He made me feel like a fool, but evidently, I was wrong."

Mel shook her head. "What? What did you say?"

Declan laughed. "I was wrong. Go ahead and mark it on the calendar. It doesn't happen often." He dropped for a kiss, but it wasn't the quick peck on the lips she'd grown accustomed to. He lingered and licked at her lips. Mel opened for him and sighed into a kiss of the panty-singeing variety. Declan lifted away slowly, twice dropping for a soft kiss. "I've got to go to work."

"But later?" she asked hopefully.

"Depends on your bum." He ran his hand down to her ass.

"My bum is as interested as I am." She only needed the donut for prolonged sitting. Thankfully.

"Then later is a go." He dropped for another kiss, and Melody lifted her fingers to her lips when he'd pulled away. God, the chemistry between them was not a problem. Declan stepped back and growled. "I've never wanted anyone more."

"Tonight," she said, and he nodded, then walked out the door. She sighed, grabbed a stack of paper, and took it to the desk. Maybe if she kept busy, the night would go faster.

A couple of hours later, Mel lifted her head from the paperwork and listened to a noise in the main bar. Oh, she recognized that braying laugh. Mel stood up and headed to the door. She opened it and stepped out to the bar. She was right. The blonde whom Declan had gone home with the second time she'd come to the bar. She was leaning over the bar top, her breasts dumping from a shirt that was opened way too far. Declan, to his credit, wasn't paying attention to her. But Melody didn't care. That woman would not have Declan again. Yes, they'd said they were exclusive, but Mel would seal that deal. She walked behind the bar, heading toward Declan, who did a doubletake when he saw her.

"Is everything okay?" He stopped pouring the beer and walked over to her, putting his hands on her hips.

"Yes." Mel put her hands on his biceps. "She's the one."

"What?" There was a furrow in Declan's brow as he tried to understand what she was saying.

"The blonde at the bar exposing her breasts to you is the woman you went home with instead of me."

Declan's eyebrows lifted skyward. "Are you jealous?"

"If I told you the cowboy was here, would you be?"

"Hey, Declan, can we get our beers?" a man standing by the bar said.

Declan glanced over to the customer. "Hang on a minute." He looked back down at her. "I would be, yes."

"That answers your question." Mel glanced over at the blonde who was shooting daggers at her.

"Okay. So, let's fix that real quick." He dropped his lips to hers and kissed her until she was breathless. The whoops and hollers in the background registered, but barely. When he lifted away, he whispered in her ear. "I'm coming home with you. Only you. We made a promise, and I never go back on my word."

She opened her eyes. "Okay."

He chuckled and winked at her. "Let me go back to work?"

"Okay," Mel said again before turning to head back to the office. She floated back to her chair and sat down. Her fingertips touched her lips, which were still tingling. She was so screwed. She'd fallen in love with Declan before she'd discovered she was pregnant. If the relationship didn't work out, her heart would be shattered into a million pieces. She put her hand over her baby bulge. She didn't want to trap Declan, but maybe she could help him fall in love with her.

Melody leaned forward and rested her elbows on the desk, propping her head up in her hands. Declan had wanted the get-to-know-you period. She hadn't suggested it, but what if she used it? She rolled her eyes when she heard that braying laugh again. A smile spread across her lips. The mule could bray all she wanted. The stud was coming home with her.

* * *

DECLAN CLOSED the doors behind the last customer. He hadn't even registered that the blonde was at the bar when Melody had come out of the office. But he'd noticed afterward. She was in his face several times. Finally, he outright told her it wasn't going to happen, that he was in a relationship.

The laughter that comment garnered from the people at the bar hit a chord, and it hit hard. No one believed he could be monogamous. Well, fuck them. They didn't know him. They only saw what they wanted to see.

"Boss, you good?" Clay Thompson asked as he took the last table's glasses toward the kitchen. "You look pissed."

Declan shook his head. "Just a long night. Put the last of those glasses in the trays, and I'll push them through before I head home."

"You got it. Oh, hey, Declan, congratulations. I hear you're going to be a dad." Clay ducked back into the galley area.

"Who told you?" Declan leaned back to see his barback stacking glasses in the dishwasher tray.

"Lord, who didn't?" Clay snorted. "Everyone in the bar tonight knew."

Declan narrowed his eyes. Everyone knew … So, did that blonde … and she still wanted to hook up? That was low. And the fact she thought he'd agree? That was even lower. What kind of man did people think he was?

A womanizer. Obviously. Declan snapped a black garbage bag open. "I'll fucking show them." He dumped smaller garbage bags into the larger bag.

"What did that bag do to you?" Mel said, drawing his attention toward her.

"Everyone at the bar tonight knew I'm going to be a dad." Declan dropped the bag and put his hands on his hips. He was so pissed.

Mel stopped. A confused look flashed across her face. "You knew that would happen."

"No, that's not the problem. That woman, whatever her name was … DeeDee, she knew." Declan pointed to the door.

Mel followed his point and then returned her gaze to him. "And?"

"And what in the hell? What type of person does she think I am? She kept hitting on me after I kissed you. She thought I'd cheat on you with her.

Jesus, what kind of person would do that? Is that how the town sees me? Without morals or character?" He ran his hand through his hair.

Mel walked over to him and put her hand on his chest. "If they do, they're idiots, and they don't deserve to know the man I know. You didn't have to acknowledge these boys. You didn't have to offer me a job, take me in, or help in any way. You're the kind of man I want these boys to grow up to be." Declan's pissed-off attitude drained from him like hot air out of a balloon.

"I'm out of here, Declan. See you tomorrow night." Clay lifted his hand as he power-walked through the bar out the front door with the garbage bags from the galley.

Declan didn't look up. "I'm not perfect. Far from it. I've been roaming, but I swear to you that I'm not looking at anyone but you." Mel's hand was warm against his chest.

"Perfection isn't obtainable. We'll figure this out. Both of us are in foreign territory."

He pulled her in and held her in his arms. "Mel, you make me want to be better. For you and the babies."

She sighed into him. "Better? No, just be yourself. That's the man I want to be with."

"Then let's finish closing and go home because I want to be with you, too." He relaxed his hold, so he could claim her lips. He didn't know how he would do it, but somehow, he'd find a way for them to move forward. He couldn't afford to lose the connection between them. Melody saw through the noise. She knew him and that he'd been loose and carefree. Hopefully, she also knew he'd meant what he said. He wanted to have a relationship with her, to build something solid for their boys. A solid, strong, and lasting relationship like his parents had.

Declan released her from the kiss, and they pulled away slowly. He managed to finish closing the bar, and Mel ran the glasses through the dishwasher as he counted out the till and filled out the deposit slip before putting the money in the safe for his trek to Belle Fourche to deposit the funds in his bank.

Declan walked through the bar, checking every room to ensure nothing was plugged in and that everything was clean. He turned off the lights and took Mel's hand. It was time to go home.

CHAPTER 10

❧

*M*el brushed her hair and stared at herself in the bathroom mirror. The scrapes and cuts on her face were almost gone, and the bruises had lightened enough that she could cover them easily with makeup. Anticipation and anxiety in equal parts coursed through her veins. Sex with Declan had always been more like an aerobic adventure. Her tailbone, for the most part, was better, and the babies were safe, but she was still a little apprehensive.

She put down the brush and stared at herself. *You tell him if he gets too energetic.* She nodded to her reflection. She could, and she would. She flipped off the light and walked out into the dark bedroom. The moonlight filtered in the window, and she could just make Declan out lying in bed.

Instead of walking over to what she'd claimed as her side of the bed, Mel pulled down the sheet that covered him and kneed up into the bed before crawling to Declan and straddling him. His hands were under the t-shirt she'd claimed for pajamas, resting on her hips. She dropped for a kiss, and Declan let her lead the way. God, the man tasted like home. Familiar, comfortable, and safe. He'd surprised her with his goodness and how he assumed responsibility. The many facets of Declan Howard were mesmerizing.

He lifted up and carefully rolled her to her side. "I missed you in this bed." She breathed the words between kisses. For the last week, he'd slept on the couch, not wanting to accidentally hurt her while she was healing.

Declan lifted onto his elbow. "It was hard to be out there. I wanted to hold you."

Mel lifted her eyebrows and laughed. "Only hold?"

He shook his head. A sexy smile spread slowly across his face. "Much, much more."

"You should show me." Mel blinked when he stood up. "Ah, what …"

"Hold on." Declan walked around the bed. "Stay like that." He slid in behind her and kissed her shoulder. "Tonight will be different." His hand slid over her waist, covering her lower abdomen before sliding up to her breast. His fingers skimmed over her nipples and sent a shiver across her skin, tightening her nipples at his command. He kissed her neck, then traced his tongue to the edge of her ear. *Oh, damn ... Holy hell ... that felt so...* Mel tightened her legs together as her sex blossomed with need and want. "So good."

Declan hummed into her ear and caused a whole-body shiver. Never had they taken their time like this. The rushed, almost frantic sex they'd had every time they'd been together was amazing, sexy, and mind-blowing. But now, God, it was on another level. Mel moaned his name, the need for him so strong it blinded her to anything else. He lifted her top leg and moved her knee toward her chest. "Is this okay?" he breathed the question into her ear.

"Yes." God, he would break her. The slow, careful touches intensified her need. Declan played her body like a master guitarist. His slow strokes, touches, and kisses acted like kerosine on the fire he had built inside her. She was wet and ready for him when he slid his shaft inside her. From behind, he undulated his hips, moving in and out of her so damn slow she reached back and grabbed his hip with her fingernails. "More." The plea was more of a demand.

"No," he whispered. "Just like this."

Mel groaned and arched as he moved forward. Declan didn't vary his speed, and the intensity still grew. She was a string stretched so tight it hurt. Then he moved his hand down toward her clit, and the second stroke of his finger over the apex of her sex caused her to shatter. Declan's hips bucked, and she heard him growl as he released inside her.

Declan moved her hair and kissed her temple. "How was that? Are you okay?"

"Never better." Mel sighed and moved back against his chest when he settled beside her. "That was … intense." She closed her eyes, feeling Declan's breath tickle past her cheek.

"For me, too." Declan sighed and moved his hand, placing it over her bump. "I'm so glad I said something in front of Zeke."

Mel chuckled. "Me, too." She put her hand over his.

The quiet spread between them until Declan spoke. "What are we going to name them?"

Mel chuckled. "I don't have any idea. Do you have any names you like?"

"Trucker."

"Veto." Mel flung back at him immediately.

"Why? It's a cool ass name."

"No."

Declan propped himself up on his elbow. "It is."

"Vetoed. Hard veto. No. Not happening." Mel shook her head.

"What name do you want?"

"What about something a bit more normal … like Lance?"

"Nope. Lance? No, you're just priming one of those boys to be teased. Masculine names like Trucker make strong men."

"Names don't make men." Mel rolled her eyes.

"They do. Do you think I'd be like I am if my name was Lance or Trey? Nope. I'd be totally different. Declan is a solid, masculine name."

"Okay, Declan Junior." Mel yawned.

"What?"

She glanced up at him. "The first one born will be Declan Howard Junior."

"You'd name one of them after me?"

"I would. Why does that surprise you?" She

turned so she was on her back and could see him better.

Declan stared down at her. "I had a realization tonight. That my reputation is how people see me. They don't know me, but they assume they do. If you'd name one of the boys after me, I'd have to change that perception."

She reached up and pushed a flop of blond hair from his brow. "These boys will be proud of their daddy. They don't need you to change. Just love them, Declan. That's all they need."

"Mel …" Declan faltered and didn't finish his statement.

"What?" She wiggled a bit so she could see him better.

"I really want these boys to be ours." He placed his hand on her bump again. "It scares me that there's a chance they're not."

"Me, too," she admitted.

"A bridge to cross when we get to it." He laid down and pulled her into him.

Mel rolled toward him and let him fold her into his embrace. Closing her eyes, she said a silent prayer that they were Declan's sons.

* * *

DECLAN SLIPPED OUT of the bedroom without waking up Mel. She needed the sleep, but he was wide awake and needed coffee. As he entered the kitchen, he glanced at the clock on the range. Ten in the morning. His usual morning since he worked late every night. He filled the coffee pot with water, put the filter in, and added the coffee. When he moved to grab a cup, he saw Ken Zorn's car heading down the drive.

Declan went into the laundry room, grabbed a t-shirt, and put it on over his jeans. Then he went to the door and opened it, stepping out onto the porch.

"Ken. What's up?"

"Dude, are you just now waking up?"

Declan nodded. "Mel's still asleep. Want some coffee?" He motioned into the house.

"Sounds good." Ken followed him into the kitchen.

Declan grabbed another cup, moved the glass pot, and stuck one mug under the drip and then the other. "What brings you out here?"

"Couple of things," Ken said after thanking him for the coffee. "Sean Goins. I can't find him."

"What do you mean?" Declan was still a bit groggy, but he was trying to keep up. Taking a seat at the table with Ken, he took a sip of his coffee and waited for the man to explain.

"When I saw that fancy car in front of your place, you know, before things got weird? Well, I took down the license plate." Ken shrugged. "You can never tell when things like that come in handy."

Declan cocked his head at his friend, considering putting a fishing hook down Ken's throat to pull out the whole story. *Maybe he needed more coffee. Probably*. He took another sip. *Yep. Definitely feeling less murdery now*. "Okay. And?"

"The car was rented to a guy who reported it stolen three weeks ago." Ken took a sip of coffee and then leveled a stare at Declan. "There are seven Sean Goins in Colorado and Wyoming. None of them match the description of the man offering you and Phil money for your land."

"How do you know?" Declan leaned forward. "Did you see him?"

"No, but Phil did. I took the pictures of the ones we couldn't rule out to him. He said none of them was the guy who came by."

"Why didn't you ask me?" Declan went back to the coffee pot, which had finished brewing, and topped off his cup. He brought the pot back and topped off Ken's.

Ken cocked his head toward the bedroom. "You had your hands full. I didn't think you needed to worry about the minutia. How's she feeling?"

"A lot better. Thanks." Declan sat back down. "What about the guy who showed up here?"

"He left for New York yesterday under armed escort."

"But he committed a crime here." Declan jabbed the table with his index finger.

"He did. After he's processed in New York for his crimes there, he'll be arraigned via video for what he did to you and Melody. He will pay for what he did." Ken sighed. "He's locked up like a vault, though. Won't say anything without his lawyer. I don't know if we'll ever know who sent him."

"Or why." Declan stared at his friend. "I can't shake the feeling that this Sean Goins had something to do with what happened. He hasn't shown his face again."

"If he does, you call me." Ken drank some of his coffee. "I've got the same feeling. The car he was driving was stolen. I think the offers he gave both you and Phil were bogus. A way to screw each of you out of your land." Ken sighed. "I guess the question would be what does your and Phil's land have in common, and why have they approached you more than they've approached Phil."

Declan nodded. "Other than we own the land and the Hollister's don't, I can't think of a thing they have in common. Phil's acreage is a lot smaller than mine. His is in the city limits, and mine is in the county."

"By a matter of three hundred feet." Ken snorted.

"Still, I'm in the county. I have no idea what the fascination with the bar is."

Ken nodded. "Well, I'll chase my tail some more on this Goins fella. If he contacts you, let me know."

"You'll be the first." Declan stood when Ken stood. "Thanks for not letting this drop."

"Well, you know my life is so full of important stuff to do." Ken laughed and stepped out onto the porch. "Right now, I need to decide what I'm going to do until lunchtime."

"I hear there's this deputy who sets up a radar trap about five miles that way. Most people think he's reading a book or something."

Ken snorted. "Books are so last year. I hear E-

Readers are the way to go. Pages don't get bent when you toss them onto the seat and respond. Or so I hear." He took off his cowboy hat and got into the car.

"What kind of books do you think he reads out there?" Declan leaned against the post of the porch.

Ken leaned back out and smiled. "I hear he's heavy into crime thrillers and spy novels. But that could just be a rumor."

Declan laughed and lifted his hand as Ken did a U-turn and drove back out to the highway. Thank God Ken wasn't researching UFOs.

CHAPTER 11

*M*el pushed herself up from the chair in the office. She'd written the check for the electric bill and put a stamp on the envelope after sealing the check in it. As she rose, one of the babies moved, or maybe they both did. They were so active. She headed out to the front of the bar, Declan saw her and opened the pass-through to the back of the bar for her. "I'm going to walk this down to the post box," she told him.

Declan took the envelope from her. "I can drop it in on the way home."

She plucked the envelope from him and shook her head. "I need the exercise." One of the babies moved again, and she grabbed his hand, placing it on her belly. "They're active today."

"It's the chili you made yesterday. That stuff was spicy." Declan put his other hand on the other side of her belly.

"It was good." She tapped him with the envelope. "I'll be back in a couple of minutes."

He bent down and kissed her while holding her belly. "Be safe."

"I will be." Declan stopped her and kissed her again before she could leave the back of the bar. Mel smiled at him as she left.

Walking out into the sunshine, the warmth of the day wrapped around her, and it occurred to her that she was happier now than she could ever remember. The light feeling dissolved the hardships surrounding her relationship with Declan. She drew a deep breath and absorbed the feeling. It was a beautiful fall day. A slight breeze fluttered the maternity top she wore. She waved at a truck that passed by. It was one of the ranchers she'd met in the two months since she'd been working at the bar and living with Declan.

The town was welcoming and wonderful. Even Edna Michaelson. Melody chuckled to herself as she walked. Edna had crowed to everyone that she knew Melody and Declan would make a perfect couple. The woman was harmless and just wanted to be involved and active. Declan's propensity to make one-line comments about suspicious activities at night while Edna was in earshot kept the poor soul chasing UFO lore.

Mel stepped up onto the boardwalk that would take her past Sanderson's store and came upon Allison leaning against the open door. "Hey, Mel."

"Hi." Mel stopped. The aroma from the store made her mouth water. "Oh, man, your mom's bread smells amazing."

Allison laughed. "I'm baking bread bowls. Gen is serving clam chowder tomorrow at the diner. Mom leaves the specialty orders to me."

Mel's stomach grumbled hungrily at the thought. "I know where I'll be for lunch." She put her hand on her belly. "These guys give me a heck of an appetite."

Allison smiled. "How are you feeling?"

"Really good. We just had our six-month checkup, and everything is moving along as it should."

Allison snapped her finger. "Oh, I wanted to invite you to Bunco."

"Buck-what?" Mel laughed. She wouldn't be riding, let alone practicing bucking off a horse.

"No, *Bunco*. It's where a bunch of us girls get together, drink a bit of alcohol, or in your case, apple juice, and play this dice game. We have little prizes for the most Buncos and the like. Nothing crazy, but girl time, you know? I told Steph I'd make sure to invite you. Not this Friday night but the following Friday. We're playing at Gen's diner."

"That sounds like fun. What time?" Mel knew Declan wouldn't mind her being gone. He wouldn't let her do anything but office work, and now that the filing was done, there wasn't a lot to keep her busy.

"Seven. We're done by nine so everyone can get home before it's too late."

"Do I need to bring anything?"

Allison nodded. "Ten-dollar buy-in that goes for next month's prizes and whatever you want to drink. Gen provides the food and usually picks up the prizes on her trips down to Rapid for the café."

"I'll be there. Thanks! I need to go post this and then get back before Declan has a cow. He worries."

"He's really changed, you know." Allison's comment stopped her.

Mel turned back. "How so?"

Allison smiled at her. "I've known Declan my entire life. He's always had a reputation as a skirt chaser. I think a lot of it when he was younger was just boys crowing out loud if you know what I mean. Declan's a great guy. Funny and a good friend. I think he was lost as he got older. Oh, he had his bar, but he didn't have anyone, you know? Steph left, and it was just him. When Steph came back, it was good for him. When you came into his life, it seemed like a switch flipped. He's the guy I remember now. He's a real good guy, Mel."

Melody felt her eyes tear up. "Oh, crap."

"Oh, shit! I didn't mean to make you cry!" Allison put her hand on Mel's arm. "I'm sorry. I just thought I'd tell you that I thought you were good for him."

"I know. You made me happy." Mel wiped at the tears that fell. "It's hormones. I'm happy; I cry. I'm upset; I cry. Two days ago, I cried because I was hungry."

Allison pulled her in for a hug. "I'm sorry I made you happy, then."

Mel laughed and hugged her new friend. "Declan bought a box of tissue for every room in the house and has one in the office at the bar and one behind the bar. It's crazy." She moved away when Allison loosened the hold.

"Who's that?" Allison stood up and stared at an SUV that pulled through town. She frowned. "Colorado plates."

"Is that a bad thing?"

"No, no. I'm a snoop. Not many people pull through the town, you know? We're a speedbump on the way north, or you can take the road southeast to Nisland and Newell. People rarely come by …" The SUV pulled up in front of Phil's garage. "Unless they need gas or their vehicle is messed up." Allison smiled. "Mystery solved."

"Okay. Well, now that the waterworks are over, I'm going to mail this and head back to the Bit."

"Have a great day, and I'll see you tomorrow for lunch." Allison lifted a hand as Mel walked backward.

"Oh, definitely. The babies are demanding it." Mel made her way to the tiny post office, put the bill in the mail slot, then went over to the Bit and Spur's box. She entered the combination and pulled out three envelopes for Declan.

After waving another goodbye at Allison on her way back to the Bit, she glanced over at the garage. Phil Granger stood with his hands on his hips, talking to four men who'd gotten out of the SUV. Back at the bar, several of the regulars were already ensconced on their usual stools. Mel said hi to each one as she passed, then handed the mail to Declan. "I'll be right back."

Declan was immediately concerned. "Are you okay?"

"Bladder." She lifted her eyebrows and headed to the bathroom. As she entered, the braying mule, as Mel mentally called the blonde, exited. The woman stopped and gave Mel a look from head to toe, then sneered and walked back to the bar.

Good Lord. Mel hurried to use the facilities, all the while mentally rolling that look the mule gave her around her brain. She washed her hands and checked the supplies in the bathroom before returning to the office. Declan was standing at the office door when she got there. '

"Need a break from the mule?" Mel asked as she approached.

Declan frowned. "I don't know what you mean. Did you get this from the post office?" He held up one of the envelopes she'd given him.

"Yep. Three letters addressed to you. Why?"

He shook his head. "Can you watch the bar for a minute? I need to make a call."

"Sure." She'd love to serve Miss Mule.

Melody went behind the bar and refilled Doc Macy's beer. "How's the county's finest vet today?" Mel asked as she took the glass and pulled back the tap to pour him a new beer.

"Busy, but that's normal this time of year. How're the boys doing?"

Mel smiled at him. "Getting bigger and feistier every day."

"As they should be." Kerry Ross said as he sat down beside Doc Macy. "Mel, can you get me one of those?"

"You got it. How are things at the plant?" Kerry ran the meat processing plant at the edge of town. He was a Wednesday night regular and didn't come in any other night. Mel poured him a draft.

"Things are slow, but that's expected this time of year. When deer season picks up, we'll be slammed. Then we'll be processing for those who slaughter cows and pigs for the winter."

Mel nodded. She hated the thought of killing the animals, but they weren't killed for sport. They were killed for subsistence.

There was a big sigh from the end of the bar. "Do you think you could waddle down here and refill my drink?"

Kerry Ross's head snapped toward the blonde. "DeeDee, you're being a bitch."

The woman rolled her eyes at Kerry. "Like I care what you think."

"You cared a week ago," Kerry shot back.

DeeDee. Huh, nah … Mel liked Miss Mule better.

"What are you drinking?" Mel asked, stopping the sniping between them, at least for the moment.

"Brandy Alexander."

Mel took the glass from the woman and put the empty glass in the wash bin. "I don't know how to make that. Either choose something easier or wait until Declan comes back."

"Or leave," Kerry said from the other end of the bar.

Miss Mule rolled her eyes. "What he sees in you, I'll never know."

Declan flipped up the bar gate. "You're right. You never will because it's none of your business. I've made it clear that I'm with Melody. I'd suggest you find another bar to drink at from now on."

DeeDee gasped and drew back. "You're kicking *me* out?"

Declan dropped his arm over Mel's shoulder as Kerry snorted from the other end of the bar. "Who said blondes weren't smart?" Kerry said. Declan looked over his shoulder and raised an eyebrow at Kerry. The man lifted his beer. "Sorry, Declan forgot you were a blond."

Everyone in the bar chuckled, and Mel leaned into the man she adored. DeeDee's mouth gaped open. She shook her head as she backed up. "You'll be sorry for not choosing me, Declan."

Declan glanced down at her at the same time as Mel looked up at him. He smiled. "Never." He bent down to kiss her. The echo of someone hitting the front door with a little too much force was the only thing that registered besides Declan's kiss.

"Hey, when you come up for air. I need my drink." Phil's voice pulled them apart.

Declan winked at her. "One draft, coming up." Declan moved to pour Phil a beer, and Mel headed back to the office, smiling all the way.

Declan sat the draft in front of Phil, who leaned forward. "I got a visit today." He spoke quietly and forced Declan to lean in. "Four men from Colorado suggested I reconsider the offer made on my property."

Declan glanced down the bar to make sure no one else was listening. "Have you called Ken?"

"Yeah, he said to meet him here. You talk to these guys?" Phil took a sip of his beer.

"No. But I got a letter in the mail today." Declan shook his head. "We'll talk about it in my office."

"Yep." Phil agreed and took another sip of his drink. He leaned back and spoke in a louder voice, "Busy in here for a Wednesday night. DeeDee left in a huff."

Kerry and Doc Macy started laughing. "What did I miss?" Phil slid off his normal barstool and headed down to the end of the bar where the others were gathered. Declan shook his head and pulled the letter out of his pocket, opening it again.

SELL THE PROPERTY, or you won't have anything.

THE LINE WAS in the center of the page. Nothing else. He pulled the envelope out of his pocket. There was a Denver, Colorado, postage stamp over the Forever stamp. No return address. His address was typed or computer printed. Nothing about the envelope or the paper made them any different than the stuff he used in his office. Damn.

He pocketed the letter again and returned to filling drinks and cleaning behind the bar until Ken walked in. Making eye contact, Declan motioned to his office, and Ken nodded. Ken spoke to everyone at the bar as he made his way over, and Declan followed him into the office after pulling Phil from his stool. Mel and Ken were chatting when he entered.

"Hey, Mel, can you watch the bar? Phil and I need to talk to Ken."

"Oh, about those guys at the gas station today? I saw them pull in when I was talking to Allison. It was really strange that they had car plates on the truck. I wonder how they don't get pulled over." Mel pushed herself up from the desk.

"What?" Ken asked.

"Oh, Colorado has different plates for cars, pickups, fleet vehicles, farm vehicles, and the like. It's easy for people who drive trucks to pick that up because, well, we see the difference. Maybe it was an honest mistake." Mel shrugged.

"Probably," Declan assured her. "Thank you." He kissed her briefly and waited until she left before shutting the door. He produced the letter and handed it to Ken, who took it out of the envelope and read it.

"Has anyone contacted you other than this?" Ken asked.

"No. Not since that fucker showed up at the house. I thought we were done with this shit. Two months and nothing. Now, Phil gets a visit from four guys, and I get a letter on the same day."

"It isn't a coincidence, that's for sure." Ken sat on the edge of Declan's desk. "Phil, what was said to you? Exactly. I'll need to get your statement ."

"They pulled up, and I walked out. I'd just gotten out from under Eric Patterson's dually. He had a hole in his exhaust, and I dropped the system and welded him on a new one. A Chevy Suburban, black, extended model, pulled in. Four men got out. These weren't guys playing as cowboys. The heels on their boots were worn, and their jeans were washed as often as any of ours. Real guys. The one driving said, "We've been sent to tell you that you need to reconsider the offer to your place. You've got three days. We'll be back.""

"What did you say to them?" Ken asked when Phil stopped talking.

"Well, I told them that they were fucking fools because Mr. Hollister had the right to first refusal for my land. If I did sell my land, I'd legally have to offer it to him first. That he'd contest the sale, and he had enough money to make sure whoever bought it was in court for a long, long time."

Ken nodded, then looked at Declan. "Did you ever mention that information to the guy you talked to?"

"No, because I wasn't going to sell. I'm still not."

"I know." Ken nodded. "All right. Well, we have more power to call in help for this now."

Declan crossed his arms over his chest. "How?"

"Threatening a person through the mail is a federal offense." Ken lifted the envelope. "Phil was threatened in person, and we have a timeline. Three days. It's time to bring in the big guns."

"The sheriff?" Phil asked.

Ken shook his head. "No."

Declan blinked and looked at Phil before he turned his attention back to Ken. "You calling Mr. Marshall?"

"I am. My gut tells me this is going to get really bad if we don't put a stop to it now." He stood up. "I'll call Mr. Marshall and see when he can meet with us and where he wants to meet." Ken looked directly at Phil. "You cannot say a word to anyone."

Phil nodded. "I'd rather cut out my tongue than say a word about this. I know I'm a fucking gossip at times—"

"At times?" Declan blurted out. Phil was nosier than Edna, but he used the information differently. As the unofficial mayor of the town, he knew what everyone was doing and who needed help.

"Screw you," he shot back. "But anything involving Guardian is locked down tight. I'm not stupid, and I'm not a fool. The missus won't even know what's going on."

"That works. Declan, the same for you," Ken warned.

Declan shook his head. "No, I'm going to tell Mel. She's a victim of this shit."

Ken pinched his lips in a grimace. "No. Not yet. Let's find out what Mr. Marshall suggests."

Declan shook his head. "I don't like keeping her out of it."

"Those babies don't need any worries," Phil said. "She stresses out, the babies stress. Keeping this from her isn't a bad thing right now. You can talk to her after we meet with Mr. Marshall."

Declan sighed. "All right. But this is on the two of you. I'm doing everything I can to make sure that woman wants to stay with me. Not telling her is *not* my idea, and I'm not happy about it."

"I'll shoulder that responsibility," Ken agreed. "Now, I want my soda."

"And I want to finish my beer." Phil snorted. "Check that. I want a cold one."

"Of course you do. To the bar, boys." Declan opened the door and ushered the men out. He hated not being one hundred percent honest with Mel, but Ken and Phil could be right. Keeping the stress from her was probably the right thing to do.

CHAPTER 12

"What's going on, Declan? Why do you want me to go to the diner for lunch without you?" Mel tried to cross her arms, but her baby bump got in the way. Instead, she flopped her arms to her sides and gave him the stink eye.

"I promised Ken I wouldn't say anything until he had a chance to work on a few things." Declan held a chair from one of the tables at the bar for her, and she sank into it.

"This involves that truck at Phil's, doesn't it?"

"It does. But that's all I can say, and you can't talk about this with the girls when you head over to the diner." Declan sat down across from her. "I swear I'll tell you everything as soon as we figure it out."

Mel stared at him. "Do you trust me?"

He blinked and sat back at that question. "I do. Why?"

She deflated a bit and bit her bottom lip before answering. "I thought you were looking into my last employer, Mr. Carrington. I mean, if those guys were trying to buy Phil's land, that's where I'd start. I thought you were trying to get me out of the bar so I wouldn't hear you discussing me."

A light switch flipped, and Declan blinked. "Holy hell, I didn't even think to tell Ken about your last employer."

Mel lifted an eyebrow. "But it makes sense, right? It's always in the back of my mind."

"It does. Can you write down any information you know about him?"

"Would you get my cell phone from the office? I have his telephone number. I can tell you where the office is and its telephone number. He paid me in cash, so I don't have any banking information." Mel ended up yelling the last bit of information as Declan hot-footed it into the office.

He grabbed Mel's cell phone, a notepad, and a pen and went back out to the bar. "Here you go."

He watched as Mel wrote the information down, then glanced at the clock.

"You need me to go, right?" Mel asked, drawing his attention back to her.

"Yeah. I'll come over and join you for lunch when we're done with the meeting." He stood and helped Mel out of her chair.

"Okay. I have towels to wash, and we need to do monthly inventory before we open this afternoon."

Declan pulled her in for a hug. "Have I told you I'm happy you're in my life?"

Mel leaned back and looked at him. "No, you haven't."

"Mel, even if you weren't pregnant, I think this, what's growing between us, was meant to be. I think destiny got it right this time. I'm happy, and I realized recently I wasn't until you came back." She teared up, but he was getting used to that, and he smiled at her. "Waterworks are open."

She rolled her eyes. "You make me so happy. I don't know how to tell you how happy I am."

She toed up, and he kissed her. "Go eat. I'll be over in a bit."

"I will, but only because the boys are starving,

and Gen is making clam chowder served in Allison's sourdough bread bowls."

Declan walked with her to the door. "Do you want to take the truck?"

Mel snorted. "No. I can walk. I'll try to save some chowder for you." She started across the parking lot.

"You eat as much as you want. I'll fend for myself if I have to." Declan lifted his voice a bit.

She turned around. "I'm as big as a house already."

"A sexy little doll house!" Declan called back.

Mel's laughter rang through the air. God, he loved that woman ... Declan blinked and stared after her. Did he love her? He leaned against the outside of the bar. Fuck, he did. When had that happened? He stared at her and shook his head. Day by day. The friendship, the concern, the worry ... all of it had intensified until he reached this point. He couldn't imagine his life without her in it now. He didn't want to, for that matter. She shined a light on a part of him he didn't know existed. He felt the warmth of loving her down to his soul.

He was still looking toward Hollister when Frank Marshall's truck pulled into the parking lot. Ken's patrol car pulled in directly behind the truck, and Phil waved to Mel as he passed her heading to the bar.

Frank Marshall wasn't the only one to get out of the truck. Andrew Hollister, or Senior as everyone called him, got out of the passenger side. Frank walked up to Declan and extended his hand. "Declan. It's been a while."

"Yes, sir, you haven't been in for your annual visit." Declan shook Frank's hand and then turned to Senior. "Sir, welcome." Senior was even less frequent of a visitor.

"Ken." Frank Marshall shook the deputy's hand. "I brought Senior along since this seemed to involve more than just my connections."

"Good idea, sir. Here's Phil." Ken tilted his chin as Phil made his way across the parking lot. "Let's go in, shall we?"

Declan opened the door, and the men filed in. "Can I get anyone something to drink? I have coffee, soda, something harder if you need it?"

"Coffee for me," Frank said.

"For me as well, if you have some creamer and sugar," Senior added.

"Soda for me," Ken said.

"Coffee, please." Phil settled on his usual stool,

and Frank, Senior, and Ken took the next three seats while Declan went behind the bar.

"I've brought Andrew up to speed on what's been happening," Frank said after thanking him for his coffee.

"The letter sent through the mail made this a federal case. Except the postal service investigators are the ones in charge of the investigation." Ken shook his head. "We have such limited resources that the sheriff mandated I turn it over to them. I've tried to track the man who showed his face and made the first offers for the land, but it's a dead end. Sean Goins obviously wasn't the guy's real name. The fancy car was stolen from a guy who'd rented it. It was found in Utah a week ago. Of course, I didn't find that out until I contacted the rental agency's fraud department this morning."

"So, we have people trying to pressure you and Phil into selling your land," Frank summarized.

"But Senior has the first right of refusal. I told them that," Phil said.

"I didn't." Declan poured himself a cup of coffee after making sure everyone had what they wanted. "The thing that doesn't fit is the attack on Melody."

"What?" Both Frank and Senior's heads snapped up.

Declan told them about the attack, then Ken added what he'd forgotten. "She was almost four months pregnant," Declan finished. "Thank God she was okay. We found out that day we were having twins."

"The man who hurt your woman, Declan, do you think his attack was part of what was going on?" Senior poured some more cream into his coffee.

"Sir, I don't know, but I just can't see how it's not related."

Frank took a drink of his coffee. "I can make some calls. Can't promise much. I just know people who know people."

Andrew Hollister snorted. "What he means is he'll make one call, and shit will get done."

Frank reached into his pocket and took out a piece of taffy. He offered everyone a piece, but there were no takers. He carefully unwrapped the piece and studied the wrapper while chewing. "Seems to me someone has their nose where it shouldn't be. Figure it's time they find out we take care of our own here in Hollister."

Ken sighed and relaxed. "Thank you, sir. I've

been chasing my tail and getting nowhere. There has to be something I'm not seeing. Something I missed. I feel like a damned fool for asking for help." Ken ran his hand through his hair.

Frank turned his head toward Ken. "You'd be a damn fool if you didn't ask for help. Lots of holes in this. Stuff don't make sense. We'll figure it out. Your woman doing okay?" He looked at Declan, who grinned proudly.

"Six months pregnant and sassy as ever. I'm a lucky man."

Frank cleared his throat. "Then put a ring on her finger, son."

Declan chuckled. "That's the plan, sir. She needs to get to the same place as I am first, if you get my drift."

Senior snorted. "Waiting on a woman."

"Not something I mind one bit," Frank said. "You need to find yourself a woman, Andrew."

"Right. Who in this country would want a withered old man like me?"

Everyone laughed because Senior was anything but withered. Broad and tall like his son, the man had silver hair but seemed ageless, just like Frank Marshall.

"Oh, crap. Hold on." Declan moved around the

bar to the table where Mel had written the information. "This guy was Mel's previous employer. He was the one who sent her out to Hollister the first time. That's how we met. She said he had buyers seriously interested in any land they could buy in the area."

Declan held out the pad, which Ken took and handed to Frank. "Out of my jurisdiction. The sheriff won't authorize me to look into it."

Frank took the piece of paper and folded it as carefully as he did the small piece of wax paper that had wrapped his taffy. "Every little bit of information helps. I assume you have a name on the man who attacked Declan's woman?"

"I thought you'd never ask." Ken opened his folio and took out an envelope. "Copies of everything I have."

Frank nodded. "Andrew, I'm going to head to your daughter-in-law's diner for lunch. You joining me?"

"Be awkward if I didn't, Frank, as you're driving me back to the ranch." Senior finished his coffee. "Both of you know I'll buy any land you don't want, but I'm never going to pressure you. This is your land. This is your community. Might have my name, but it's your town. I'll do anything to help it grow."

Frank finished his coffee and stood up. "Andrew, I believe you like to make speeches."

Senior rolled his eyes. "Better than grunting."

Frank looked at him and grunted. Declan laughed as the two old cowboys left the bar while Ken sighed and downed his soda. "You don't get any better men than those two."

Phil nodded. "Salt of the earth. People you want your kids to grow up like. Ken, give me a ride back?"

"You got it." After they headed out, Declan cleaned up. Then he grabbed his keys and locked the door. As he walked over to the diner, he decided he needed to become a person like Mr. Marshall and Senior. Not ranchers, but salt-of-the-earth type people. He wanted his boys to be proud of him. He'd been toying with the idea of taking college classes online and thinking about remodeling and maybe expanding the Bit and Spur. It was time to put the desire to become what he wanted to be into motion.

CHAPTER 13

el looked at the booth and then decided a table was a better idea. She slipped into a chair a second before Edna Michaelson came into the diner with two of her friends, Belinda and Doris. Mel had met the ladies before but never really talked to them. Edna was usually the one who talked for all of them.

"Melody. How are you today?" Edna sat down, and the other ladies took the other chairs at the table.

"Ah, fine … Declan is on his way over for lunch." She felt a little closed in and sent Gen a look over Edna's head.

"Oh, we've got our booth. We'll move when he

gets here, but we've been thinking that you need a baby shower."

Gen made her way over to the table. "I agree, Edna. I've been planning one with Stephanie. Maybe we should work together on it." Gen poured Melody water from a big ice-cold pitcher.

"A baby shower?" Mel's jaw dropped. The thought hadn't crossed her mind.

"Why, yes! You'll need two of everything. Gen, me, and the ladies were thinking of asking around for cribs and such. We can repaint them to match and get new mattresses and bedding and such."

Gen smiled widely. "That's a wonderful idea. A changing table and maybe a dresser, too?"

"Wait, we don't even have a bedroom for the babies." Mel felt like she was caught in a jet stream or something. Things were moving fast, that was for sure.

"Sure, you do. Have you been to the old place?"

"The old place?" Stephanie walked into the diner with Zeke.

Edna nodded. "Melody was saying they don't have room in Declan's house for two cribs and all the stuff the twins will need. Your parent's house is right there."

Stephanie nodded. "Yeah, but it'll need to be

cleaned from top to bottom. I started it, but it's been sitting vacant again for over six months. And the porch needs to be fixed."

Zeke shrugged. "I can grab a few of the guys, and we can get that fixed in one day."

Edna clapped. "If we show up in mass with buckets and cleaning supplies, we can whip the house into shape in no time. We can even paint the nursery."

"What about the old heater?" Stephanie shook her head. "Babies need it to be warm in the winter. I don't know if Declan got the heater fixed."

"I can take a look at it," Carson Schmidt said from one of the booths. "Tegan is good with things like that, too. When do you want us to come out?"

Mel's head jerked from person to person. "Wait, Declan needs …"

Edna flopped a hand in her direction. "Declan needs to make sure you and the babies are taken care of."

Two more tall cowboys with silver hair walked in. "Hey, Mr. Marshall. Senior. Have a seat. I'll be right there. We're talking about fixing up the old place out at the Howard's so Declan and Melody have room for two babies. His newer house is more of a bachelor pad." Gen moved to go over and pour them cups of water.

"The heater is the long pole in the tent," Zeke said. "From what Declan's told me, it is on its last leg."

"Got a heater for a structure that ain't getting built until next summer. You could have that." Melody gaped at one of the gentlemen who had just come in. Mr. Marshall, she thought his name was.

"I'll swing by on Saturday to pick it up," Carson Schmidt offered.

"No need. I'll have one of the men bring it over. That and the fixin's, ductwork, and stuff in case you need it."

Mel was about to hyperventilate. Oh God, she had no say in any of that. What would Declan think about moving out of his new little house back into the big house across the small field? She couldn't agree to any of it without talking to him. She leaned forward to look at Mr. Marshall, "That's so kind, but …"

"No buts." Edna stood up. "Frank, you're a saint. Okay, this is the plan. Spread it along to everyone you know. We'll meet out at the Howard's place Sunday after church. Buckets,

KRIS MICHAELS

tools, supplies, you all know the drill. The ladies and I will find us two old cribs and such and start stripping them down."

* * *

DECLAN ENTERED THE CAFÉ, which was in a state of turmoil. Mel turned as Declan walked in. He cocked his head and mouthed, "What's happening?"

"Declan, there you are. Come in. Ladies, to your booth." Edna clapped her hands together.

Mel reached out for Declan as he approached. "I swear to you, none of this is my doing."

Stephanie and Zeke sat down with them, and everyone else settled into booths, the bar, or the two tables Gen had wedged into the small front of the café. "She's right. She just got swept along with the tidal wave," Stephanie shared.

Declan put his hand over hers. "What happened? Why are you upset?"

"They said baby shower, and then, somehow, it turned into everyone is going to come and clean out the old place and paint, and that man gave us a heater for the house, and I didn't do a thing, and I'm so happy." Everyone watching seemed to smile and turn away at that last part. Tears ran down Mel's face, and Declan pulled her into him and held her. He sighed and looked over at Stephanie and Zeke.

"It happened just like she said. You *will* need room for the babies. We're all coming out on Sunday to fix up the old place and get everything working." Zeke smiled at Corrie, who came out of the kitchen with a tray of bread bowls and clam chowder. "Lunch. I love chowder day."

Declan kissed the top of Mel's head. "Sweetheart, it's okay. This town is amazing, and we're going to take them up on their offer to help. When someone else needs it, we'll be there for them. It's what we do."

Mel nodded. "It's so nice."

"I'll come out with food. Gen, can I use the diner to cook up something?" Corrie asked from one end of the diner.

"Great idea. I'll meet you here before church, and we can get everything going." Gen hustled from one table to another, taking drink orders and pouring water.

"I'll have cold refreshments," Declan announced. There was a round of cheers from everyone. He'd tap a keg and have sodas and water available.

Declan kept his arm around Mel, and she leaned into him. The buzz in the café was all about what each could do to help out. He smiled and kissed the top of Melody's head. With all its quirks and slightly insane people, this town was the best place on the face of the earth. There was nothing that a neighbor wouldn't do for a neighbor. And it looked like Sunday, he and Mel were the target of its generosity.

CHAPTER 14

rank pulled his truck up to the new communications building on the Annex side of the ranch. He got out, shut the door, and mounted the steps. It was a rare occurrence that the people of Hollister reached out to him for help. Rarer still that they wanted help, not from him, the rancher, but for his connections to Guardian.

That Guardian was on his ranch was the best worst-kept secret in the world. Not one of those folks in Hollister would act like they knew what you were talking about if you asked about Guardian. Not one of them. Yet they accepted Guardian as one of their own and didn't ask questions.

Mike White Cloud met him at the door. "Hey, Frank. I was just heading over to the house. Anything you need from me?"

"Nope. Going down to see Jewell for a minute."

"Roger that. I'm out of here, then. See you later." Mike walked on by as Frank headed down the hallway and used the retinal scanner to open the elevator into the secure complex.

He heard Zane laughing before he hit the communications node. After entering the code, he walked into what looked like a popcorn party …

"Hi, Dad!" Jewell laughed. "We decided to have popcorn as our treat for the week, right, Ethan?"

"Well, you decided." Ethan ducked as Jewell reached around to smack him.

"Fine, you decide next week." She bounced over with a bag of cheese popcorn in one hand and caramel popcorn in the other. Jewell hugged him, and he hugged her back. That she called him Dad was an honor he'd never take for granted.

"What brings you down to the bat cave?" Zane asked. "We have two who are truly batty." He laughed and caught a piece of popcorn that Ethan tossed his way.

"I was hoping to get some help for the people of

Hollister." Frank pulled out the envelope and the piece of paper he'd been given.

Jewell put down the popcorn bags and grabbed her chair. "Anything. What do you need."

"Not sure. We have a person or persons who're trying to muscle two of our town's people out of their land. One got a threatening letter after he refused an offer that was way too high for the land, and the other was visited by four men. Threatening, if you get my drift."

Jewell nodded. "What information do I have to work with."

"Phillip Granger is one of the landholders. The other is Declan Howard."

Jewell's fingers flew across the keyboard. "What else?" she asked, looking at him while typing. Impressive.

"It might not be related, but Declan's woman used to work for this guy. She didn't have a lot of information about him, but he was in real estate and told her he had buyers for any land for sale in this area. He sent her out this way, and that's when she and Declan met."

"All right, I have Granger and Howard's land records. They're current on taxes, and there are no loans against the land."

"This is the license plate of a car used by the person who made an offer on Declan's place. Ken Zorn told me it was reported stolen and recovered in Utah, and this is the letter Howard received."

"Cool. I'll work on this. There has to be a connection between Granger's land and Howard's."

"I can start work on the car." Ethan reached for the pad.

A shrill sound stilled both of the people at the keyboards, and Jewell looked over her shoulder. "Sorry. That's a priority Shadow request. This will have to wait until we can get back to it."

Frank nodded. "Work it when you can."

He got no response from Jewell or Ethan, who were both typing furiously.

"I'll try to sneak it in as soon as possible. They don't usually get breaks like they did today. We were having some fun," Zane said as he grabbed a bag of open popcorn and rolled the top down, putting a paperclip over the foil to keep it fresh.

"Son, you take care of those two however you need to do it. Here's some more information. That man beat on a pregnant woman and then lawyered up. He's from New York and was just taken back there to face charges pending against him. This request isn't a priority, but it is a big concern. Someone's trying to muscle people in Hollister, and I don't cotton to it at all."

Zane nodded. "I understand, sir. Those people have been good to us. We'll work it."

Frank watched the screens scrolling and flashing on and off. "They're amazing."

"Brilliant in the most unique way," Zane agreed.

"I'm going to miss you when you head to your mountain." Frank liked having his family there, but it was for the best to have people scattered in undisclosed locations.

"At least Ethan will still be here, and Jewell and I will be back. Often." Zane chuckled. "You and Miss Amanda mean the world to us."

"As you do to us. Let me know what you find out."

"I will." Zane sat down in a big chair at the back of the room as Frank let himself out of the communications node. He'd check back. He wouldn't let this sit under a snowbank for too long. Ken Zorn was right. Something smelled like three-day-old dead fish toasting on a patch of cement during the hottest days of summer. Foul.

CHAPTER 15

*D*eclan woke slowly. Melody was on her side and bumping up against his semi-stiff cock. He snuggled into her a bit more, and she purred a response and pushed back into him. "Good morning."

"How did you sleep?" They'd made love just about every night since his talk with Zeke. This was their favorite position. It supported the babies, and he could make Mel shatter.

"Good. I only got up twice to pee. I swear one or both of these little guys think it's funny to bounce on my bladder."

"Are you ready for today?" He ran his hand up under his t-shirt that she loved to wear and placed his hand on her stomach. One of the babies moved, and he could feel the little guy as he flipped or flopped. "I'll never get enough of that." Declan laughed.

"I love it, too. Except when they land on my bladder." She rolled to her back, and Declan helped prop her up on an extra pillow. She put both hands on her belly and shook her head. "I'm never going to see my toes again, am I?"

Declan lifted his head and looked down at her feet. "They're still there."

She snorted. "So not the point."

"You look beautiful." He stared at her for a moment. "I figured something out yesterday."

Mel rolled her head on the pillow and looked up at him. "Yeah, what's that? Oh, you mean the meeting you had. I forgot about that after the diner incident."

Declan chuckled. "No, there was nothing settled at that meeting. But I did have a revelation after you left for the diner."

"Yeah, what's that?"

"That I'm in love with you." He stared down at her as her eyes grew wide and filled with tears.

"You are?" He nodded and dropped for a kiss, his hand still on the babies. One of them kicked as they kissed, and Declan broke away with a laugh. "They don't like to share you."

"Declan, are you sure?" Mel's voice was tiny and scared. He hated that.

"I am. Do you think you could ever love me?"

"I do. Not think I love you, but I do love you." Mel reached up and cupped his face in her hand.

His cell phone vibrated on the bedstand as he bent down to kiss her. He wanted to remember that moment in vivid detail. But the phone shattered that thought when it vibrated again and again. Declan pulled away. "Damn it."

She chuckled. "Answer it. I need to get up anyway." She tipped her head toward the bathroom, and Declan helped her roll into a sitting position. When she was on her feet, he reached for his phone without even looking at the number. "What?"

"Hey, man, we're loading up, and then we'll be on our way over. I know you guys sleep in, so I wanted to make sure you had time to shit, shower, and shave before the entire town descends on you," Ken said.

Declan groaned and looked at the clock. It was later than he'd thought. "All right. Thanks, man."

"No worries. Do you need anything before I head out?"

"No. I have the keg in the chiller, and we have enough cleaning supplies to sink this part of the state."

"You ain't seen nothing yet." Ken chuckled. "See you soon."

Declan got out of bed and made it before Mel was out of the bathroom. She looked at the bed. "So, we're not going back to sleep?"

"The whole town will be here in just a few minutes." Declan pulled her into his arms. "I don't want you to overdo it today."

"I won't. I'm going to try to stay out of Edna's way." Mel laughed. "She's called me at least twenty times. They have paint for the nursery. She didn't even ask what color we wanted it." Mel chuckled. "Something tells me it will be midnight blue with UFOs painted on the ceiling."

* * *

MEL STOOD in the doorway of what would be her boys' nursery. Disbelief at the room's transformation shocked her into stillness. The walls painted a pale green, and someone had also painted a tree on one wall with squirrels and raccoons, along with colorful birds and rays of sunshine dappling the leaves. She lifted her hand to her mouth as she walked in. Dark green cribs were against opposite walls. They had brightly colored birds on the headboard and footboard. A dresser and a changing table were also painted dark green. One had a raccoon, and the other two squirrels scampering down the drawers.

"Oh. It's beautiful. How did you do this in one day?"

Edna came in behind her. "Belinda found the mural stuff. It's stickers. You can pull this all off when the boys get older and they want super-heroes or something."

Mel turned to find the very shy older woman almost hiding from her. "Miss Belinda, thank you so much. They're absolutely perfect. I adore it." The woman blushed bright red and ducked her head. "Thank you, ladies. I don't know how you managed it in such a short amount of time."

"Edna," Doris Altham spoke up. "Edna is the driving force behind everything we do."

"Well, thank you, ladies, and thank you, Edna. I'm blown away by your kindness and generosity."

Edna preened a bit. "We rely on each other

around here. Little things like this don't cost a whole lot … Well, unless you donate a furnace and such, but it allows people to give what they can and feel like they contributed. The ladies and I are working on blankets and such. They'll be crocheted and knitted. That'll take longer. We normally meet once a week to work on things like that."

"How can I ever repay you for all you're doing?"

Edna smiled brightly. "Be there when someone else needs help. We all pitch in, right, ladies?"

There was a chorus of agreement. "But we've got a few things to touch up in here, and there's a splotch of paint we need to get up off that hardwood floor. You don't need to be around any chemicals, so go visit with the others, and we'll finish up here."

"You're staying to have something to eat and drink, right?" Mel smiled. "Declan brought home two bottles of Chardonnay, especially for you ladies."

"Well, you couldn't beat us away with a stick." Edna laughed. "Now, go, so we can finish."

Mel thanked them again and made her way through the house. Everything was spotless. The floors were pristine, and there wasn't a speck of dust in the entire building. New curtains hung in the living room. Kathy Prentiss, one of the teachers at the school, brought her sewing machine and hemmed them to the right length. Even the rugs were new. Stephanie had declared the old ones had given their all. She and Zeke had bought the rugs and new curtains and paid for all the lumber to replace the wood of the wrap-around porch. All day today, the sounds of power saws, hammers, and laughter punctuated the music playing. Mel walked outside and saw Declan and the men gathering around the keg.

"Over here." Steph waved her over to the new rocking chairs set up on the porch.

"This one is for you," Gen said as Mel stepped out. "I'm grabbing some beer for us. What can I get you, Melody?"

"Nothing, thank you. I just had a bottle of water." Gen smiled and hopped off the porch, heading toward the men and the keg.

"I'm dumbfounded. This is amazing." She pushed the chair and relaxed into the motion of the rocking. "Oh, this chair is the best."

"Eden said that you'd love it. She and Jeremiah got them for you as housewarming presents."

Stephanie pushed her chair, too. "This house was full of love when we grew up."

Mel glanced over at Declan. "It'll be full of love again."

Stephanie turned to look at her. "Do you love him? Wait, you don't have to answer that. I'm being nosey."

Mel chuckled. "I do love him. He told me he loves me, too." Those words had blossomed into a feeling that filled her very essence with happiness.

"Good. I'm glad." Stephanie put her hand on Mel's. "I know I didn't take it the best when you and Declan broke the news to us, but I'm so happy for you and for him. He's like a different person when he's with you. He used to try to be my protector. You know, big brother and all that, but with you ... I see the man he was meant to be. It's like the other half of him stepped forward. When he's with you, he's complete. Does that make sense?"

Mel nodded. "That's how I feel. When I was waiting for him here, the night of your engagement party, I was terrified. I'd lost my job; my family was of no help." She saw Stephanie's questioning look. "Oh, that's a long story, and I'm going to need a drink to tell it, so let's wait until after the boys are born."

Steph reached for a beer that Gen handed her. "What did I miss?" Gen sat down on the new deck cross-legged.

Steph took a sip of beer. "Mel is going to need a drink to tell us about her family."

Gen rolled her eyes. "*Pah-lease* do not talk about family. My mother is coming to visit."

Stephanie spat out the beer she was drinking.

"Eww … Holy crap, Steph," Gen moved and wiped off her arm on her jeans.

"Sorry, so sorry. How did I not know this?" Steph put her beer down and cleaned herself up. "When?"

"I just found out about it this morning. Dad is trying to head her off, but if he can't, next month sometime."

"I thought they got a divorce?" Steph picked her beer back up.

"Yep, but he still keeps a tight rein on her. He still has leverage. She wants his money and connections so she's under control for now. I don't know what I'm going to do if she does come up."

"Your mother sounds like a winner. Mine is

right there with yours." Mel nodded and kept the chair rocking.

Gen chuckled. "When you can drink again, we'll compare notes."

"Can I come? My mom is a saint, but I'd love to hear the stories." Allison sat down with Gen on the new porch. "The attic is clean as a whistle, and everything Steph said shouldn't be thrown out is stacked neatly. I may have been lost in your family's photo albums for the last thirty minutes or so, Steph."

"I need to go through those and make two books, one for Declan and one for me." Steph pushed herself on her rocker. "Not today, though. I'm done."

"You all should be done. You worked like crazy," Mel agreed.

"It's so much easier when there's a bunch of people to help," Gen said as she watched Edna lead the procession of gray-haired warriors toward the men.

"What are they getting up to?" Steph asked.

"Declan brought two bottles of wine for them."

"He didn't bring wine for us, but he brought wine for them?" Allison snorted. "I'm insulted. Aren't I?"

Gen shook her head and laughed, "Do you like wine better than beer?"

"Ah, no, but you know, I feel like I should be insulted. Ah-oh … there's going to be trouble …"

Mel watched as Carson Schmidt snuck up behind Ken Zorn and poured a bucket of water over him. Ken's shocked face and the dance he did try to get the ice out of his shirt sent Mel into a giggle fit.

He stripped off his shirt and snapped Carson with the wet material while Edna fussed at both of them, calling them delinquents. As the older women moved toward the porch, Corrie came around the porch and hollered, "Dinner's ready!"

Mel waited for the other women to get up and accepted Stephanie's assistance getting out of the rocker. She glanced back and watched Allison, who was looking at Ken like a dog looked at a piece of prime rib. Mel nudged Stephanie and nodded at Allison. Steph leaned over. "Girl, that's a long history and one hell of a stubborn woman. I'll fill you in later." They walked around the house, and Melody smiled. Four picnic tables were adorned with red and white checked tablecloths, candles, and mason jars full of wildflowers.

"Pregnant women first!" Corrie directed Mel to

the front of the line. There were two tables full of food.

"This looks amazing." Declan jogged up to her and put his arm around her, then whistled loudly.

When he had everyone's attention, he cleared his throat and began, "I've been to events like this with y'all before. I never understood the emotion in the recipients' voices the way I do today. Mel and I are starting a family, maybe a bit out of order, which we'll correct eventually, but we wouldn't have been able to do what you've done for us today. Hollister is more than a community. We're family, and we thank you from the bottom of our hearts."

Mel listened to the responses and smiled. She'd become part of their family, and she was so blessed.

CHAPTER 16

he day had been surreal. Declan had pitched in where he was needed and handled all the clean-up and heavy toting. The old furnace was ripped out, and Carson and Tegan installed the new one. Both men had already left, but he'd made sure to thank them. Ken, wearing one of Declan's shirts, was gathering up his tools and getting ready to leave as he said, "Hey, I didn't get a chance to tell you that Frank called Saturday. He said it was a busy time, but the information we gave him would be worked when they could get to it."

Declan handed Ken his hammer and responded, "I figured it would be a lower priority.

The seventy-two hours that Phil was given has come and gone."

"I spent the entire day and most of yesterday tucked back and waiting. Phil had his shotgun handy the entire day." Ken shoved his hammer into his tool bag. "I do not want to arrest that man for killing someone."

"It would be justified, though," Declan baited Ken.

"Justified or not, I'd have to go through the motions." Ken looked up, and Declan's smile must have given away the fact that he was teasing. "Anyway, dork, if you hear anything, let me know. I'll do the same."

"Sounds like a plan, and thank you for everything today." Declan grasped his friend's hand and pulled him in for a quick bro hug.

"You'd do the same for me." Ken grabbed his ball cap and put it on. "I'm going to go grab a shower, a beer, then get some sleep. Monday always comes around too early."

Declan lifted a hand as Ken headed to where the vehicles had been parked. With Ken's departure, only Zeke's truck was left.

He made his way to the old place and stepped up onto the porch. Zeke had pulled two folding lawn chairs out of the bed of his truck, and the girls were in the rockers that had appeared from somewhere. Declan kissed Mel and lowered himself into one of Zeke's chairs.

"Today was impossible and amazing." Mel sighed. "I've never seen anything like it."

Zeke chuckled. "When Hollister was hit by a tornado years back, it was like this but on a continuous and massive scale. Jeremiah ended up coordinating the effort for rebuild, and he also built the clinic we have now. This little town will make good come from just about every event if you give them long enough."

"You know, you could move in now. Everything is done and ready." Stephanie rocked back and forth slowly. "Do you remember sitting out here with Mom and Dad?"

Declan nodded. "Dad had that Welsh voice. He'd sing on nights like these. Everything would stop. The bugs even listened to him." Declan glanced over at Mel. "He could sing a unicorn down from the sky."

"Unicorns don't exist," Mel reminded him.

Declan smiled. "They do if a Welshman is singing and the air is still enough for his songs to make it to heaven."

Stephanie chuckled. "Daddy was full of those sayings. But I got sidetracked. Zeke and I would be glad to help you move everything over tomorrow. We don't have any patients until two in the afternoon."

Declan looked at Mel. "You feel up to it?"

She bit her lip. "Are you sure you want to? I'm good staying in your house until the babies are born."

Declan took her hand. "I built that house across the way because I didn't want to live in this one by myself, and it gave me a project to work on when I wasn't at the bar."

"Because he was always at the bar." Zeke chuckled.

"At one point, I was sleeping there," Declan agreed. "That little house was a project to keep me busy. It has one bedroom and one bathroom. The kitchen is the size of my office at the bar. I don't have a problem moving over. There isn't much to move."

"Good. Then we'll be over about eight tomorrow morning," Steph said and yawned.

"Make it nine. Everyone needs to sleep in," Mel agreed as Stephanie's yawn spread around the group.

"Perfect." Zeke sighed and stood up, offering Stephanie a hand. "Take me home, woman. I need a hot shower."

Stephanie took his hand and stood. "We should conserve water."

Declan groaned. *Oh, God, really?* "No. No, no, no. Go away. I don't need to think about my sister getting dirty in the shower."

"Getting clean." Stephanie laughed. "Clean all over."

"Stop it! Gah, I'll never get that out of my head." He shuddered.

Zeke laughed and bent his knees, getting low. Stephanie hopped on his back, and he hefted her up piggyback style. "See you tomorrow."

Declan grabbed Mel's hand as the couple laughed their way to the truck. Stephanie squealed in the darkness, and then there was silence for a good two minutes before Zeke's truck door opened.

"They're good together," Declan said as he lifted a hand when the headlights illuminated the darkened porch.

"She said that about us today." Mel continued to rock. "Everyone was so wonderful."

Declan squeezed her hand. "We should get you to bed. You look wiped out."

"Can we sit for just a while longer?" Mel asked, toeing the chair again.

"Sure." Declan sighed and relaxed into the canvas seat. "The nursery looks great. No UFOs, though. I told Edna I was upset."

Mel's head snapped around. "You did not."

Declan chuckled. "I did. She said we should look closer. So, I figured she's hidden one or two in there."

"You're the worst to her." Mel sighed, rolling her eyes.

Declan shook his head. "Nah, you see, she wants to have something she can dig into. The things that happen around here are too common-place, and even though she's a busybody, she's a good person. Her heart's right. With the UFO thing, she gets big adventure instead of small-town drama."

Mel hummed a noncommittal sound. "If you ever think I need big adventure, would you please refrain from assisting me?"

He laughed and lifted their joined hands, kissing the back of hers. "I promise. Besides, I think both of us will be busy for the next eighteen to twenty years."

Mel rubbed her belly. "I'm scared."

Declan was dead serious in a heartbeat. "About what?"

"Am I going to be a good mom? Will I flake out like my mother did? I don't have the loving family background you and Stephanie did. What if I screw it up?"

Declan got out of his chair and knelt down in front of her rocking chair. "A lady I know and happen to love once told me all we have to do is love them."

Mel grunted. "I love them already. But I want to be a good mom. Not like mine. I want to meet them at the bus stop and have afternoon snacks ready for them. Have birthday parties with ponies and bouncy houses."

Declan put his arms on the arms of the rocker and stopped it. "Nothing says you can't be that kind of mom."

"She was always busy with her boyfriends. She loves me, at least I think she does, but not enough to be there for me." Mel sighed. "I want to be there for my babies. And I don't want her to have anything to do with them or us."

"What brought all this up?"

"She called today. I was in the little house, using the bathroom. Again." She rolled her eyes. "She wanted to know if I'd gotten you to fess up money for child support."

"But the babies aren't born yet." Declan didn't think child support started until there was, well, a child to support.

"She wanted money, Declan. She wanted to know where I was. Wanted to come to visit." Mel sighed. "I hung up on her." She looked up at him. "I don't want her to poison what we have. I don't want her near the boys. She'll steal, lie, and con anyone to get what she wants."

"Then she isn't welcome here." Declan leaned in. "You're not your mom. We'll make mistakes, that's pretty much guaranteed, and we won't have riches, but we'll have each other, and we'll have a lot of love."

The tears started to flow. Mel sniffed. "How do you always know what to say to make me happy?"

"A natural talent, I guess. Now, let's get some sleep. We're moving tomorrow."

"Is it technically moving if it's on the same property?" Mel asked as he helped her out of the rocker.

Declan considered that as they made their way to the newly built steps. "Relocating is probably a better word."

Mel nodded. "What was your mom like?"

Declan sighed, smiling. He slowed their pace down a bit so he'd have time to talk. "My parents were older. Mom, in my mind, always had gray hair. She helped my dad ranch right up to the end. She was my safe place. When I couldn't talk to Dad, Mom would be there, and she'd let me talk it out. She never judged me but had a way of asking those questions that put me on the right path to figuring things out. Dad was strict, but he was fair. Though we never had a lot of money, we had enough. Summer evenings were spent on that porch. Dad would spin stories or sing, and Mom would make popcorn every weekend. We caught fireflies and played ghost tag as Mom and Dad sat here and laughed. It was a good way to grow up."

"I hope our boys will have such fond memories." Mel leaned into him.

He dropped her hand and put his arm around her shoulder. The night song of crickets formed a background as he glanced back at the old place. He could almost picture his parents on the porch. "I'm sure they will, sweetheart. I'm sure they will."

CHAPTER 17

❦

*M*el walked into the diner and stopped dead in her tracks.

Blue balloons and crepe paper streamers were pinned to the ceiling. Gen, Stephanie, Corrie and Ciera Evers, Kathy Prentiss, Allison and her mom Karen, Edna and her posse, Phil Granger's wife Sarah, and Maggie Patterson, who ran the post office and beauty shop, all yelled, "Surprise!"

"What?" Mel looked from the ladies to the presents to the cake. "What is this?"

"Your baby shower!" Stephanie clapped her hands. "Allison said she told you it was Bunco. That was ingenious."

"Yeah, we don't play Bunco, but after Allison described it to us, we thought we would start a monthly game," Edna explained. "Come in, woman. We have games and presents and this." Edna's crew moved, revealing a beautiful rocking chair painted in dark forest green with brightly colored birds at the top of the chair. There was a fluffy dove gray cushion tied to the back and the seat. Mel stopped and looked at the ladies she knew were responsible for the rocker. "This is beautiful!"

Edna preened. "We saw the rocking chairs that the Wheelers gave you and about kicked ourselves for forgetting a rocking chair for the nursery." Edna's crew all nodded in unison. "So, we found this in the secondhand store in Belle and were able to get it stripped and painted in time. Belinda got the material for the cushions, and Kathy sewed them up. She's a wiz with that sewing machine."

"It wasn't hard." Kathy chuckled. "A rectangle and a square with zippers to add the poly filling. Add a couple of ties in the seams, and poof. Done."

"I know it had to be harder than that. Thank you, Kathy and ladies, you are spoiling me." Mel sat down in the rocker.

"Everyone deserves a bit of spoiling every now and then," Mrs. Sanderson said. "Allison, you were in charge of games. What do we have?"

Mel laughed as Allison explained in detail how everyone needed to tear off a piece of toilet paper to the size they thought would go around Mel's belly. She'd never seen women take a game so seriously.

Obligingly, she stood up and lifted her arms as people measured their length of toilet paper. Gen won and apologized over and over for tearing such a long strip of paper. Mel thought it was hilarious. She knew how big she was getting.

"Okay, okay, here's your gift, Gen." Allison handed her a box wrapped in blue paper. Gen unwrapped it and showed off two sets of baby blue booties.

"I don't think I can use these." She sat them at the table by Mel's chair. "I bet you can."

Mel opened her mouth to object, but Allison interrupted her. "Let's have some cake and punch, and then we'll play the next game." Allison herded everyone toward the cake. "Melody, you get to cut it."

"It's too pretty to cut! It had to take hours to decorate."

Ciera Evers chuckled. "I'm getting quicker at it. I loved making the booties on the top. They are marshmallows tooth-picked together, and then I frosted them."

"They're adorable. Thank you so much for this. Can someone take a picture?" Mel reached for her phone and handed it off. The women were hilarious, and Mel laughed so hard she had to pee. The night progressed as they played a memory game where Allison showed a tray with baby items and people had to list what they'd seen.

Edna won that game and received bibs as her prize. "I'm not old enough for bibs yet." Edna winked at Mel as she placed them on the table.

The next game was to pin the sperm on the egg, and Mel felt sorry for Gen's wall. The pin marks would be visible. No one was close, but Allison finally won by feeling along the wall after they spun her until she found the poster board where the egg was drawn. She gave Mel the pacifiers she won. Then they started the "Don't say baby" game before Gen brought out a big washing tub on a wheeled cart. She pulled off the tablecloth and announced, "Bobbing for pacifiers!"

Mel laughed so hard. When Kathy Prentiss finished first by trapping the last three pacifiers in her mouth and beating Maggie Patterson's time, Kathy opened her prize and gave Mel a set of baby bottles. Of course, three people were eliminated from the "Don't say baby" game by saying "baby" in front of bottles.

"Okay, okay, ladies, we need to settle down and open up the real gifts." Gen took charge of the party. "But we're going to have some fun as Melody opens her gifts. We have Baby Shower Bingo. Use the candies on the tables, and when the gift is unwrapped, if you have that item on your bingo card, cover it up. The first to bingo wins …" Gen lifted bottles of Chardonnay and Merlot. "These don't go to the babies."

A cheer erupted from the women. "Okay, Mel, first one."

Stephanie sat down beside her. "I'll write down who gave it to you and what it is so you can write a thank you card."

"Thank you. I have pregnancy brain some-times." Mel accepted the first gift. It was wrapped so pretty that she took her time and was careful not to rip the paper or the bows. "A baby monitor. No, two monitors."

"You're out." Edna laughed at Mel. "Don't say 'baby.'"

Mel laughed, "I forgot we were playing!" She smiled at Gen. "Thank you so much."

"You're welcome." Gen handed her the next gift.

* * *

AT NINE-THIRTY, the party broke up. Mel hugged everyone and thanked each of them. Stephanie, Allison, and Gen stayed behind. "I'm going to need to call Declan to get this home," Mel noted.

"Nope." Gen shook her head. "It's Friday night, he's busy, and I've got my truck. We'll put all this in the truck, and I'll take you to the old place. It's right on my way home. I can handle the rocker and the presents. It won't take but a second to unload."

"And less than that to load it up because we're all going to help," Stephanie added.

"I feel like I've said thank you at least a million times tonight," Mel said with a smile.

"I think you have." Allison snorted. "But, girl, it was so much fun. We had a blast planning it. So, thank you for giving us something to do other than the ordinary day-to-day."

Stephanie nodded. "We had a blast. Come on, let's get this loaded."

"I'll call Declan and let him know Gen is taking me home." Because no one would let her lift a finger—that had been proven over and over throughout the evening.

As she dialed Declan's number, she watched as the three women loaded a wheeled cart that Gen had and headed to the back of the café.

"Did you have fun?" Declan answered, his voice holding a hint of laughter.

"You knew?"

"I knew," he admitted.

"I had a wonderful time. They gave me so many presents for the babies."

"That's what a baby shower is about, isn't it?"

"Well, yes, but I want to show them to you. Gen will take me home on her way out to her ranch. If I fall asleep, wake me up when you get home?" She couldn't wait to tell him about the night.

"If you're sleeping, I'm not waking you up. You and the boys need your rest. I'm glad Gen is taking you home. Things are hopping here tonight, so it'll be late. I love you, and I'm glad you had a good time."

"I love you, too." Mel sighed and hung up, then turned around to three smiling faces.

Allison sighed. "I want that someday."

Gen pulled her friend into a hug. "You will, sweetie. You'll find it."

Steph put her arm through Melody's. "Ready to go home?"

"Home," Mel repeated. "Yes. I'm ready to go home." She wanted to put the baby's things in the nursery, sit in the room in the quiet, and be thankful for the wonderful friends she'd made.

CHAPTER 18

"Where's Moe tonight?" Clay asked as he returned from the galley with another tray of clean glasses.

"His sister is getting married down in Kansas. He's gone for two weeks. Visiting family." Declan poured three more drafts and a pitcher for a table out front.

"You want me to take those to the table?" Clay offered.

"I don't want to lose my license, so no." Declan laughed and picked up the tray, taking the beer to the table. "On your tab?" he asked Tegan and his crew.

"Please. I'll be up there to settle up soon. These

guys may be good to drink all night, but I'm too old for this shit."

Tegan's co-workers jumped on that statement like a pack of dogs fighting for a steak bone while Declan just shook his head and headed back to the bar. Old Man Perry poured himself off his stool, and Declan caught him as he staggered. "Who's picking you up tonight, Cab?"

Cab Perry blinked up at him. "Drusilla."

"What time is she supposed to be here?" Declan walked Perry to the door.

"Here now. Texted me."

Declan opened the door and looked for Dru's truck. She flashed the lights, and he waved at her as her dad made his way to the truck. Ever since Cab's wife had passed on, he'd become a regular. Hopefully, that would end soon, but he'd give Cab a couple more weeks before he mentioned anything to the guy. He couldn't imagine losing Mel. After living with and loving someone for most of your life, man … he didn't want to think about it.

Declan poured drinks, broke up one fight, tossed two no-accounts out for hassling some of the local girls, and kept up with the tabs. A typical Friday night, but usually, Moe was working with him. Clay kept the tables bussed and the glasses clean. Declan gave all tips to Clay. The kid was worth his weight in gold, and he deserved a little bit extra. It wasn't a huge amount of money by any definition, but it gave the kid some spending money.

As the crowd thinned, Declan turned down the music and lifted the lights a bit. The regular crowd knew that meant last call, and those who weren't regulars figured it out. Declan poured the last drinks and made sure everyone who had too much had a way home.

Declan started cleaning the bar as the regulars nursed their last drink, and Clay caught up with the glasses in the galley. The dishwasher was old, but it was a workhorse.

"Hey, Declan."

Declan felt his shoulders drop. *Fuck.* He turned around. "DeeDee. I believe we agreed you needed to find someplace else to drink from now on."

DeeDee wore an almost-there shirt and make-up thick enough that he could probably use a spatula to scrape it off. What had he seen in her? Compared to Mel, DeeDee was chopped liver. And he didn't like liver, chopped or otherwise.

"I was wondering if you could give me a ride

home?" DeeDee dragged one of her long fake nails across the wood of his bar. "I'd make it worth your while."

"Nope, no can do." Declan crossed his arms.

DeeDee's eyes narrowed. "You should have said yes." She turned and glanced at the last of the people in the bar before looking over her shoulder. "Closing soon?"

"You know I am. Look, DeeDee, we're never going to happen again. I'm in love with Mel, and we're starting a family. You should fish in deeper waters."

DeeDee chuckled. "I already am." She lifted her hand and wiggled her red-tipped fingers at him before she and her double-jointed hips swayed exaggeratedly as she exited the bar.

"She's trouble. Always has been." Riley Popham snorted. "Saw her down in Belle last weekend. She was hooking up with trouble. Four guys. They were over her like bees on honey. Her mom's probably rolling over in her grave."

Declan snorted. "Her mom's alive and lives up in Buffalo."

Riley tossed back the last of his drink. "Well, you know what I mean. I'll see you later, Declan. Tell Melody I said hello."

"You know Mel?" Riley wasn't a frequent visitor at the bar. He owned a small place south and east of Hollister, about halfway between there and Newell.

"Met her once when she was here months ago. Nice lady. Glad you two are together." Riley put on his cap and headed toward the door. As Declan watched him leave, a tiny green monster peeked over his shoulder. Jealousy, something he'd never felt before, tucked its claws into his back and held on. It wasn't a pleasant feeling. He may have used a little bit too much force to wipe the bar as he continued to clean while the last of the stragglers headed home.

Clay took out the trash and had the last of the glasses queued up and ready to run through the dishwasher by the time Declan had counted out the till. He was in his office when Clay tapped out for the night. Declan took a sip of the coffee he'd poured for himself and reviewed the paperwork that needed to be done. He listed the amounts of which liquor he needed to order, and he wanted the distributor to add another keg of the pale ale to the delivery. The customers had taken to the new beer.

Declan pulled out the ledger and the money

bag. He and Mel would drive down to Belle in the morning on Sunday and deposit the week's income, have lunch, and do any shopping that needed to be done. He put the money, less the till's starting total, into the deposit pouch. Declan placed the till money in a separate envelope and put it in the small safe he had bolted to the floor.

He stood up and grabbed his keys. That was when the smell of smoke hit him. A thread of outright fear shot up his spine as he dashed out toward the galley. There was nothing wrong there, and the dishwasher wasn't running. The last load was done. He moved quickly to the front of the bar. Where was the smell coming from?

He looked up and saw smoke. The roof. Damn it.

Declan went into his office and opened the fire suppression system cabinet. He turned the key and hit activate. The panel didn't light up like it did when the salesman had done the demo. He darted out to the bar. Nothing. Declan raced back and made sure the key was in the right position, then hit the button again. Nothing. He moved on to single system activation buttons. *Nothing. Nothing. Nothing.* Fuck!

Declan ran to the bar where he kept his cell

while working. It wasn't … He searched around and under the little shelf where he kept his phone. Where was it? Where was his phone? No one had been behind the bar or … DeeDee … that fucking bitch. His cell phone was always on that shelf right by the bar. Right where she'd been when his back was turned to her.

Declan ran for the landline. No dial tone. He hit the cradle hook several times, praying for it to connect. No such luck. It was dead. *Son of a bitch.* Declan shot to the front door. He could sound the alarm using his truck's horn. It would wake someone in town. He hit the door on the run. The doors didn't move. He shook them. Fuck!

He ran to the emergency exit. The bars on the inside depressed, and he pushed hard with his shoulder. No movement. Holy hell. Declan reared back and kicked the doors. Nothing. Someone had to have jammed something through the handles. He shot to the back door by the galley. It was rarely used but functional. He unlocked the deadbolt and tried to open it. No movement. He reared back and kicked it with all his might. Nothing. It wasn't going anywhere.

The windows. Declan opened the window in his office. The crossed iron bars over the window would take forever to remove. Same for the supply room that he fucking reinforced after Zeke had broken through it during the winter. Only there was nothing he could do with an opened window on this side of the bar. He was facing away from the town. Nothing but blank acreage this way, and he could scream until the cows came home. No one would hear him. The bathrooms were facing the same location, and there was no way he'd fit through the small windows at the top of the wall. Fuck, fuck, fuck!

Declan flew into the bar area and grabbed his tool kit from under the bar. He'd have to unscrew the bottom bolts on the metal bars at the office window.

The smoke was billowing, and there had to be visible signs of fire now. Someone could notice, but Declan couldn't count on it. The town rolled up the sidewalks at dusk, and most people were asleep by ten. Fuck. He glanced at his watch. One in the morning. The likelihood of anyone being up now was next to nothing. Even Clay would be home. Shit.

Declan shook out the tools and found the wrench he needed. He glanced back at the bar to see black smoke filling the area. Declan ran to the storeroom, grabbed two bundles of bar towels, ran water over them in the galley, and shut the door to his office. He put the towels at the base of the door and started on the bolts to the window. It was his only prayer for getting out alive.

His knuckles were torn and bloody by the time he got two of the bolts off. He was coughing. The smoke was invading his office.

"Declan!"

He grabbed the iron bars. "Here! I'm here!"

Scott Evers bolted around the bar. He didn't have a shirt on. "The doors are barred, and I can't get out."

"Hold on!" Scott ran back the way he'd come. Declan continued to work on the bolts. A flash of light appeared seconds before Scott's truck launched over the cement barriers that formed the gravel parking lot. The truck slid to a stop in the dirt. Scott got out and grabbed a tow strap from the back of his truck.

Declan helped him weave the strap through the metal bars. "Get back!" Scott yelled. Declan saw the flash of blue lights as he moved away from the window. Scott's truck yanked forward, and the bars groaned. Scott put the truck into reverse and backed up to the wall of the bar.

Declan saw the reverse lights go out and heard Scott slam on the gas. The truck catapulted forward, and the bottom of the bars bent. "Whoa, whoa, whoa!" Declan yelled. He ran to the window and went headfirst through the window, snaking out of the hole. Scott unwrapped the tow strap from his truck and grabbed Declan by the arm, half-dragging him to the truck. They got in, and Scott tore across the empty land. They turned wide, and that was when Declan saw his bar. It was totally engulfed in flames. A huge plume reached skyward. His storeroom, which was right beside his office, had gone up in smoke.

Declan stared at it, not seeing Ken, who had driven up beside them. "Declan! Your house is on fire! Follow me, Scott!"

Declan held on as the man beside him drove like a bat flying straight out of hell. "Fuck! Mel's there."

"Hold the fuck on." Scott's foot slammed against the gas pedal as soon as they hit the pavement.

"Hold on, baby. Hold on!" Declan repeated the words over and over.

CHAPTER 19

*M*el woke up with a start. She'd heard something. Had Declan come home? There were no lights on, so no, it wasn't him. Well, whatever woke her up didn't matter now. She had to pee. As much as she enjoyed being pregnant, the constant need for a bathroom was not fun. She rolled and pushed herself upright, rubbing her belly before she stood up. She padded across the bedroom and used the bathroom, almost falling asleep on the toilet.

"You're a mess, girl," Mel said to herself. She opened the door to the bedroom and blinked. A yellow glow from outside was illuminating the bedroom. Had Declan started the camping lantern? He'd done that a couple of times that week when they were sitting outside. They'd install outdoor lights when Tegan could come help wire them. Declan could build about anything, but he wasn't good with electricity, and Mel didn't want him to electrocute himself, so she'd agreed to wait. She went through the house and opened the door.

Instead of seeing Declan on the rockers with a camp light, she saw his house engulfed in flames. A truck turned in a wide arc, and the headlights blinded her for a minute. But it didn't stop. It sped down the drive toward the highway.

Declan! Oh crap. Mel hurried back into the house and called Declan. "He doesn't want to talk to you now." The bray of Miss Mule's laugh shocked her into inaction, and Mel stared blankly at the phone.

She hung up and called 911, reporting that the house was on fire, all the while praying that Declan wasn't with that bitch. Mel hung up the phone and went back outside. The fire had hopped to the bushes beside the house.

Shit. It was so dry that the fire could spread to the old place. Mel put on a pair of cowboy boots and went to the side of the house for the hose. She turned on the spigot and started dousing the ground as close to the fire as she could stretch the hose. Tears filled her eyes from the smoke or the thought of Declan with that woman. She couldn't decide which. The little house groaned loudly, and part of the roof fell in. Mel kept spraying water.

"Mel!"

She turned around at the sound of her name. Declan was running toward her. His face was covered in black soot. She dropped the hose, and he scooped her up. "Thank God, oh, thank God." He held her as she hung onto his neck.

"She said you didn't want to talk to me."

"Who?"

"The fucking mule!"

"DeeDee? She stole my phone from the bar tonight. Someone locked me inside, and they torched it."

"The bar?" Mel tried to understand. "Oh, my God. How did you get out?"

"Luck and a damn strong tow strap." Declan walked toward the old place. "What were you thinking, fighting a fire with a garden hose?"

"I wasn't fighting the fire. I was trying to keep it

from our home." Declan lowered her into the rocking chair on the porch. He knelt in front of her and pushed her hair away from her face.

"Baby, by definition, that is fighting a fire." He leaned in and kissed her.

"You could have been killed tonight." She grabbed hold of him and hung on.

"So could have you," Ken said as he stepped onto the porch. "There are metal shims under the door handles. Anyone inside couldn't have gotten out."

"She knew. She knew I could have been in that house, and she laughed." Mel felt her insides drop. "Dear God, how could someone do something so vile?

Ken's head jerked around. "Who knew?"

"DeeDee." Declan coughed hard. "She stole my phone from the bar. The landline was cut. All the doors were blocked. Scott Evers used a tow strap to pull the iron bars back from my office window. That's how I got out."

Melody watched as the volunteer fire department arrived on the scene. The big hose from the tanker truck saturated the area around the house, stopping the possibility of the fire from spreading before it turned to extinguish the flames of the small home. She held onto Declan as he lifted her from the rocker and took the seat with her on his lap. Obviously, neither one wanted to separate. He was holding her as tightly as she was holding him.

Ken prowled the deck and talked on his cell phone. "Frank Marshall called. We'll have visitors at about ten tomorrow morning. Make that this morning. They were flying out before I made the call to Frank to let him know what happened.

"What about Phil's garage?"

Ken shook his head. "Nothing that I'm aware of." He glanced at his watch and then at the fire truck where the men were congregating. "Yo, Phil!" Ken whistled, and Phil swung around.

He jogged across the field, saying as he arrived, "We got a call about the bar. It's gone." Phil shook his head. "I'm sorry, Declan."

Declan nodded, which Mel could tell because she felt him move as she held onto him. "The fire suppression system didn't work. I tried everything to make it engage. It didn't."

Ken nodded. "Phil, did you happen to drive past your place on the way here?"

"No, took the most direct route. Why?"

"Let's head back to town and make sure your

place is good to go." Ken nodded to his patrol car. "I'll follow you in."

"Fuck." Phil ground out the word. He glanced up at her. "Sorry, Mel."

"I agree with your choice of wording, Phil. No need to apologize."

"I'll be back. Phil, let's get there and check things out. Mel, do you have your cell phone?"

"Yes, in the house. The kitchen."

"I'll call that if I need to get ahold of you, Declan. I'm sorry shit has come to this," Ken said, and both he and Phil turned away.

Declan started the rocker as the fire truck, and the men who followed it started to leave. Father Murphey, the head of the volunteer fire department, made his way over. "We've put it out. There may still be some embers, and it might flare back up. You should keep an eye on it for the next twelve hours or so."

Declan nodded. "Thank you."

Father Murphey nodded. "You took a heck of a blow tonight, young man. Remember, God is good all the time. This, what happened tonight, was done by men. Cowardly men. Be strong in your beliefs. You'll come back out of this series of events stronger. I'm here if you want to talk." The man smiled sadly and headed back to the fire truck.

Mel leaned into Declan's chest as he rocked. She stared through the darkness at the little house. "She didn't know we'd moved. She thought I was in that house."

"She'll pay for what she's done tonight."

"I could have gotten out through a window," Mel mused. "I'm pregnant, not an invalid."

Declan rubbed her arm. "No more firefighting, though."

"I was so stunned when she answered your phone."

"Did you think I'd cheat on you?" Declan continued to rock. His hand rubbed up her arm and down with the slow movement of the rocker.

"I didn't want to. I think I went into survival mode. I prayed a lot." She tipped her head up. "Are you Catholic?"

He blinked and looked down at her. "No, why?"

"Father Murphey. I just assumed."

"No, he's just a good man trying to make sense of this like everyone else."

"Why would someone do this?"

"I don't know." Declan was quiet for a moment. "Riley said hi."

213

Who? Mel looked up at him. "Riley who?"

A bit of a smile flashed across Declan's face. "Just a guy." Mel sighed and adjusted, snuggling closer to the man she loved. She closed her eyes, exhausted.

*D*eclan carried Mel into the bedroom and laid her down on the bed. She was wearing his t-shirt and a pair of cowboy boots. The woman was fearless, squirting water on the ground in hopes of stopping the fire from spreading. Almost seven months pregnant and fighting fires. He drew a deep breath and pulled off her boots, sitting them at the foot of the bed. Then he pulled a blanket over her and headed back outside. He managed to get outside before he coughed again. He'd inhaled a lot of smoke.

The image of that flame as the storeroom caught fire flashed through his head. He would have been dead if Scott Evers hadn't been there.

He'd have to look the guy up and thank him again. Then the sight of Mel so damn close to the fire. He hadn't even waited for the truck to stop before he'd hit the ground running.

He walked over to the small house he'd built with his own two hands. There were small bits of glowing material. Thankfully, there was no wind, and the ground was saturated from the fire hose. The roof was partially collapsed. Windows had shattered, and he saw what Ken was talking about. A four-inch-wide piece of metal was wedged under the door handle. It would have kept Mel inside the house. Rage like he'd never known filled him. They'd tried to kill him, Melody, and his unborn children. If he saw DeeDee before Ken found her, she wouldn't live to see another day. And that was coming from a man who'd never hurt a woman. Never … He shook his head. Never say never.

He saw the headlights against the little house but didn't turn around. It was Ken. He'd said he'd be back. The lights turned off, and he heard a door shut a moment before Ken stopped beside him. "Phil's garage was broken into. Most of his tools were stolen. They trashed the inside. It will take some muscle to clean up, but he has insurance, so he should get the tools replaced."

"She can't get away with this."

"She wasn't the only one. No way that woman did the damage to the garage or jammed that metal into place." He nodded toward the piece at the front door. "How's Mel?"

"Sleeping." Declan shook his head. "They tried to kill all of us."

"Who are they?" Ken rubbed the back of his neck. "I'm grateful people are coming out to assume this investigation. The sheriff called and told me to secure the scenes until the feds showed up. I'm assuming that means the people Frank said were coming."

Declan nodded and looked around. "The sun's coming up."

Ken sighed. "It looks like it's going to be a good day to catch the fuckers who've been messing with us."

Declan turned toward his friend. "If I see her first, it won't be pretty."

"Don't go hunting no trouble, and that reminds me, I'll need a statement from you and Mel."

Declan tipped his head toward the old place.

"Let's get some coffee, and I'll write one up for you. I'm not waking her up."

"Can't say as I blame you." Ken walked with him across the field. "It's a good thing you moved to the old place."

"Who's watching the bar?" Declan said as he went into the kitchen and turned on the light. He held up his hand and tiptoed through the front room and into the hallway, closing the door to the back of the house. He went back into the kitchen, where Ken was pouring water into the coffee maker.

"Scott Evers. He told me he just happened to wake up and saw the fire out the window that overlooks the street. He saw your truck still parked there. Threw on some boots and hauled ass."

"He saved my life." Declan sat down at the kitchen table. "Fuck."

Ken opened the refrigerator and pulled out a dozen eggs. "Yeah, I've been repeating that word a lot tonight." He sighed, then asked, "You said the fire system you put in didn't work?"

"Not in the slightest. I followed the instructions. The system is self-contained. I paid an arm and a leg for it."

"I remember when you had it installed. Do you remember who did the installation?"

"Pearlman Fire Outfitters from Rapid. I fucking followed the instructions. I might have lost the roof, but I shouldn't have lost the bar." Declan dropped his head back and closed his eyes. "I lost the bar."

"But you didn't lose Mel, and you didn't lose the babies." Ken cracked some eggs into a bowl. "Positives."

Declan realized what Ken was doing. "Are you making breakfast?"

"I am. I'm starved, and you will be, too, once that shock wears off."

"Shock." Declan blinked. Yeah, he probably was in shock. He couldn't concentrate. His mind hopped from one thing to the other. He was raging mad one second, depressed and desolate the next before he bounced to being so very thankful Mel was okay with the next thought.

"Well, probably not the right medical term, but I've been around enough people that have been through trauma. You'll bust out of that haze you're fighting your way through." Ken looked around. "Frying pan?"

"That cabinet." He pointed to the one Ken

needed before he got up and went to the fridge. He pulled out a slab of bacon and handed it to Ken.

"Now you're talking." Ken reached for it. "Why don't you go take a shower? You're kind of … sooty."

Declan glanced down at his arms to see they were lined with a black residue. The knuckles on the back of his hands were torn into hamburger meat.

"You need to have Zeke look at your hands. How did that happen?"

"Trying to undo the bolts on the iron cage that covered my window, I had three done, but I wouldn't have gotten out in time. As Scott pulled away, the fire reached the storeroom." Declan continued to stare at his hands.

"Declan."

He jumped and looked at Ken. "What?"

"You kind of zoned out on me. Go shower, and I'll make breakfast and drink your coffee."

"Right." Declan nodded and headed back to the bedroom and the shower. He felt like his feet were dragging through clay. It would be one hell of a long day.

Mel was still sleeping as he made his way through the bedroom and into the bathroom. He stripped and turned on the shower, then caught a glimpse of himself in the mirror. His face was streaked with soot and grime. Around his nose, the soot was darkest, which was probably why he was coughing.

The water cascaded down on him, and he closed his eyes, drawing in the warmth. He wasn't sure how long he stood under the shower before he felt a cold draft as the shower door opened. He opened his eyes as Mel stepped into the shower.

"I smell bacon." She moved up to him and kissed him.

"Ken's making breakfast." He wrapped his arms around her.

"Oh, good, that gives me time to do this." Mel grabbed the soap and told him to turn around. He closed one eye and looked at her.

"I don't get to take care of you very often, Declan. Let me do this today." He bent down and kissed her, then turned around. She washed his shoulders, digging her fingers into the tight muscles and working them. God, her hands felt wonderful. He braced himself against the shower wall.

She soaped her hands and worked his back like she'd worked his shoulders. "Turn around."

He was a pile of goo, boneless and exhausted. He turned around and bolted wide awake when her soapy hand grabbed his cock. She kissed him when he started to object. "Let me take care of you." Her hand worked his shaft, the soap and warm water making the sensation sexy as fuck. He'd never had anyone give him a hand job before, but holy hell, he'd let Mel do whatever she wanted. He wrapped his arms around her, and their tongues danced as she worked his shaft. He didn't try to prolong anything. He let her march him straight up that slope, then swan-dived over that cliff. He braced himself with one arm against the shower wall while holding her with the other.

When he could open his eyes, the most beautiful picture in the world stared back at him. Mel's smile was bright, and he could tell she was happy. "That feel good?" she asked, blushing from her chest to her cheeks.

"Damn good," he admitted. "I love you, Mel."

"I love you, too."

She waited for the kiss he slowly lowered to give her. "Then marry me."

She gasped and jerked away. "What?"

"I almost lost you and the babies last night.

Marry me." He dropped his arm from where he was bracing himself and held her.

She lowered her eyes. "Declan …"

"What?" He tucked his finger under her chin, lifting her gaze.

Once again, the waterworks were flowing. He wiped one of the tears with his thumb. "What, baby?"

She drew a shaky breath. "There's the possibility that these babies—"

"Stop right there." Declan dipped so she'd look at him. "I don't care if those babies were put in your belly by aliens. They're mine. I'm going to love them and raise them as mine. No one will ever take you or these kids away from me." He swore to that with every iota of his being.

She leaned into him and started crying in earnest. He held her and rocked her under the warm water. "We're going to be a real family." She swiped at her face, which was puffy and splotched red and the most beautiful sight in the world.

"We are." Declan sighed. "You'll have to wait for a ring and a fancy wedding. Everything I had except you, the boys, and this house went up in smoke last night."

Melody shook her head at him. "I don't need a

ring or a fancy wedding. You, me, and the justice of the peace. I'll help you rebuild the Bit and Spur. I'll be there with you through all of it."

He stared at her and knew she meant every word. "All I have to give you is love."

She whispered, "That's all I'll ever want."

CHAPTER 21

*D*eclan sat on Ken's bumper as the insurance adjuster from Rapid City circled what was left of the Bit and Spur. He'd called early that morning, and the man had zoomed up to Hollister as if he didn't have any other clients. "Your policy indicates you had a fire suppression system."

"It didn't work."

The man grunted. "It was new."

"It didn't work," Declan repeated.

Ken crossed his arms over his chest. "You do realize he was locked inside the bar when it was set on fire, right?"

The adjuster nodded. "But you managed to escape."

Ken chuffed. "Mister, you sound like you think Declan set fire to his bar."

"The insurance coverage is hefty. One would think excessive."

Declan gave a disgusted laugh. "You tell that to the feds." He nodded to the black suburban that pulled up in the parking lot. Six men exited, and he recognized one. Jared King. He stood up.

Jared stopped about halfway to them and pointed to what was left of the Bit and Spur. He motioned, and the men went to work. Then he walked over to where Declan and the others stood. "Deputy Zorn." He extended his hand. Declan was still glaring daggers through the fucking insurance adjuster. Jared caught the vibe immediately. "And you are?"

"Lonnie Delt, insurance adjuster."

"Huh. Well, Mr. Delt, I hope you didn't touch anything."

"Excuse me?" The man lifted his eyebrows past almost past his hairline.

"My name is Jared King. I'm the Chief Executive Officer of Guardian Security." Jared reached into his suit pocket and handed the man a card from what looked like a gold-plated card holder. "We've assumed this investigation."

"An arson? Why is Guardian taking a torch job?"

Jared cocked his head. "What investigative agency did you attend to qualify you as an arson investigator?"

Mr. Delt jerked back. "I haven't."

"Then why don't you let my experts determine what happened here and at the other location."

"The other location?" Mr. Delt snapped his gaze to Declan.

"Do you have a card, Mr. Delt?" Jared looked at him expectantly.

"I do." The man pulled one out from under the clip of his clipboard.

"Good. I'll ensure you get our report after all criminal apprehensions have been made. We wouldn't want any information to be disclosed prematurely." Jared smiled at him. "Good day."

Declan lowered his head to hide his smile. God, he'd love to have the power to shut some power-hungry asshole down like that. Delt puffed out his chest. "I'll be sure my superiors know about this."

Jared literally rolled his eyes. "Oh, please do, Mr. Delt. Please, do. Now, if you'll excuse us, we have an investigation to complete."

Declan watched as the man stomped off in a

huff, his phone to his ear. Delt opened the door of his midsized sedan, threw his clipboard into the passenger seat, and slammed the door shut.

Jared sighed, "One in every crowd. Now that he's gone, let's get down to business. Ken, would you go get Mr. Granger? Frank and Mr. Hollister are on their way in. We have some information, some actions that have been taken, and I want my fire investigators to go over both sites with a fine-tooth comb."

"The fire suppression system didn't work," Declan repeated. "I did everything by the numbers, and it didn't work. It was a self-contained unit. I had it installed not too long ago. It should have worked." His mind was stuck on that point. He'd been proactive. The Bit was his livelihood, and he'd protected it.

Jared turned and whistled loudly. His inspectors all lifted as one. "The suppression system didn't work. Find out why."

"On it," one of the men acknowledged before they all went back to work.

"I'll go get Phil." Ken got in his SUV and drove to where Mr. Delt was parked in his car. He honked, and the man jumped. Ken rolled down his window. "You need to move; this is a crime scene."

Jared King chuckled. "I like that guy."

"He's a good friend." Declan rubbed the back of his neck. "Mr. King, DeeDee Hillier, she was in on this. She took my cell phone from the bar so I couldn't call for help. The landline was cut, and when Mel called me last night, the bitch laughed at her. DeeDee thought Melody was in the house. Her truck was parked outside, and until last weekend, we *did* live in that house. The town got together and helped bring the old place back up to livable standards. We're having twins, and the house I built was tiny. If we hadn't moved … God, I could have lost them." A shiver ran through his body. His mind was still spinning, and he was on pins and needles. The adrenaline spike just seemed to get higher and higher. The free fall wasn't ending, and he had no idea where a parachute was to slow the events. He was fucking lost.

Jared nodded. "That's something we'll talk about as soon as everyone is here." Jared stared at his people as they worked. "You could have been killed, too."

Declan sighed. "It was a close call." He held up his hands. The backs were no longer black with soot, but they were mangled. He'd have scars on top of scars. Zeke had looked at them that morning and cleaned and wrapped the damage when he'd brought Mel in for an exam. He wanted to make sure the stress of last night hadn't hurt her or the babies.

"All the doors were locked from the outside. I was trying to get the bars off the window in my office. Scott Evers—he's Ciera Evers' husband, she works at the café, and they live above it—he saw the place was on fire and that my truck was still parked here. He pulled the bars off the window with his truck and a tow strap."

Jared nodded. "I know, Scott. He's a damn good man. Who's with your wife now?"

"We aren't married yet. She's at the clinic. My sister's fiancé, Zeke Johnson, and Dr. Wheeler are in the building. So is Eden Wheeler; she's a nurse practitioner. I wanted her to do a check to make sure everyone was okay. Melody decided that fighting the fire with a garden hose was a smart thing to do last night."

Jared chuffed a bit. "I know Zeke, Jeremiah, and Eden as well. People in these parts are made of tough stock."

That was true, although right then, he felt as helpless as a kitten with its eyes closed. He stared at the bar.

He wasn't law enforcement, nor was he a Guardian, and he wasn't anyone's idea of a hero. But he was a man in love, and he swore by everything holy he'd protect Melody and his sons, even if that meant tracking down the bastards who intended them harm on his own.

Declan saw two trucks heading their way. One he recognized as Frank Marshall's. The other was Andrew Hollister's. They pulled up and shook Jared's hand while Ken and Phil parked beside their trucks.

"I'm sorry I can't offer you anything to drink this time," Declan said as everyone gathered.

"Looks like you have other worries," Frank said as he stared at the destruction.

Declan huffed. God, was that the understatement of the century? "Yes, sir. That I do."

"Hopefully, I can address the majority of your concerns," Jared said, taking over the conversation. "Frank, we worked on the information you gave us. I'm sorry it took so long, but some of our operations had to be completed before we were able to devote time to this."

"Understandable," Phil said, and Declan agreed, nodding his head. The bar was his life, but it wasn't anything but a blip on the screen for an organization as big as Guardian.

Jared turned to face the men from Hollister. "Let's start from the beginning. Melody was sent here to find out information that she could obtain about you, Phil, and you, Declan."

"What?" Phil frowned and sent a questioning glance toward Declan.

Jared held up a hand. "We ran her boss at the time to ground. He's an ex-con with two strikes against him already. He told us he was trying to hustle some work with investors interested in land in the area. He sent Melody out, and she gave him nothing more than he already knew. She didn't do anything wrong. But when he wanted her to go back and try to get more information, she quit."

Declan nodded. "That's what she told me."

Jared nodded. "Carrington, her ex-employer, provided us information on the entity looking for land."

"Why do they want grazing land?" Senior asked.

"That's just it. We've discovered they don't want the land. They want the mineral rights for this land." Jared lifted his eyebrows as the group digested that information.

Declan shook his head. "I don't even have well water under this acreage. What minerals?"

Jared pulled out a map that was printed on an eight-by-ten piece of paper. He handed it to Mr. Hollister first, but they all gathered around to look at it. "This is a copy of the map Carrington had in his possession and happily shared with us."

Senior shook his head. "Oil? Nah, we've done a few prospect wells back in the day. They didn't find anything."

"With the hit in North Dakota, people are speculating due to the composition of the land and the similarities in mineral makeup that there's oil here, too. And they want the land bad enough that they're willing to beat up a pregnant woman, burn down your bar, and vandalize your garage." Jared's words caused everyone to look up.

"Who are we talking about here?"

"There are so many layers to this, but ultimately, it flows back to a Chinese contingent. There are shell companies in front of them, and on the surface, it looks like an American company, but our computer specialists followed whatever electronic breadcrumbs they could and tracked it back to this conglomerate of people. They have known terrorist ties, or Triad ties, if you will. They're systematically buying land. Declan, with your land, they could exploit all the land around it. Same with you, Phil."

"What about the ranches farther south?"

"Carrington said the land changes as you go farther south. They're concentrating their search in this area. There could be millions of gallons of crude underground. At least, that's what they're banking on."

"What can the government do about this?" Senior asked.

"That's now firmly in the lap of the Department of Homeland Security. They have the latitude to react in ways we can't."

"React?" Declan didn't understand what Homeland could do.

"Seize the land that was purchased," Frank clarified for him.

Oh, well, damn. But he still didn't see any closure here. Declan crossed his arms. "It wasn't a Chinese contingent that torched my house. DeeDee Hillier was in on it."

"I received that information from Ken last night. I put out a pick-up order for her through federal channels. She was arrested this morning in Wyoming and transported to Rapid City. I'll be going down to interview her and the two other men she was arrested with."

A sharp whistle interrupted their conversation, and everyone looked over at one of the inspectors. "Excuse me for a minute, gentlemen." Jared walked over to the inspector.

Hollister handed the map to Phil, and the man snarled at the paper. "They trashed my place and stole from me. But I can still pump gas and work on smaller things until my insurance comes through. I have a bit put aside, too. We'll be okay, but they took your livelihood from you, Declan."

Declan nodded, his head hanging low. He looked up at Ken and then at the others. "My insurance agent was pretty damn sure I set fire to my own bar and tried to kill myself. I don't know if I'll ever see a penny of that money."

"Delt's an idiot." Ken shook his head. "An idiot with a pen and an attitude. I agree. It could be a long time before you see the money."

"Lawyers can sort it out, but I have a feeling Guardian's report will put a spur to the man's ass. Until then, I'll front you the money you need to get by and rebuild." Frank said as he looked at the burnt-out shell that used to be the Bit and Spur.

"Sir, I can't let you do that." Declan had no idea

what he would do, but he'd manage. Get a job in Belle or something.

"You can. I'll make it legal. Tally and payback. That keeps it a business proposition. The only thing I'd ask is, if you have the inclination, you add a hall or a party room with a separate entrance from the bar. A gathering place other than the church's multipurpose room. It's good, but not big enough for wedding receptions and the like."

"A place for town parties, like on the fourth of July," Senior agreed. "Or Christmas tree lighting and such."

"That would be good. You know, so the ladies would be more willing to participate. Some don't cotton much about going into a bar. Nothing against your bar, though. I loved it," Phil added.

Declan stared out into the acreage he owned. "I could do that and build a barbeque area off to one side. Covered with a roof to keep the sun and rain off. Not to serve food or anything, that's Gen's market, but for those occasions that the town wants to gather."

Frank handed him a piece of taffy. "That sounds mighty fine."

Jared came back, his hands in his pockets. "The sprinkler system was a self-contained system."

Declan nodded even though Jared hadn't asked a question. "It wasn't charged. There was nothing in the system to extinguish the flames. There was no chemical trace in the pipes, no water residue, which there would have been even after a fire. I'll need the name of the company that installed it. My investigators will be doing some digging on that issue, so Mr. Delt has no questions unanswered."

Declan rubbed his forehead as he told Jared the name of the installer. Exhaustion draped over him like a wet blanket. The heaviness was wearing him down. "What else can go wrong?"

"Don't ask that," Ken begged him. "Please, don't ever ask that."

"Amen," Jared agreed. "So, we have two men who managed to avoid us. We have their names from Carrington. That's how we arrested the two with Ms. Hillier. Carrington hired them on behalf of his contact in Denver. We're tracking down that angle, too, and it will be an ongoing investigation. Hopefully, it won't involve any of you."

"The other two, do I need to worry?" Declan asked. "I can take Mel to Belle Fourche or something. Find a house for her." Anything to keep her and the babies safe.

"Those two? No, we'll apprehend them, they

aren't that smart, and we're deploying assets to make sure they're found. My concern is repeated efforts by this contingent to run you off the land. But others within the organization are working on that."

Frank slowly unwrapped his taffy. "What you got in mind?"

Jared stared at Frank and seemed to consider his words carefully. "We're going to send a message via channels to which we have access. They won't like the message, but I believe they'll back down. We'll be keeping tabs on the players. They're known to us. We have eyes on the people who pull the strings and more than a few of the puppets."

"What about DeeDee?" Declan might be out for blood, but he wanted to know that she would reap what she'd sown.

"Right now, she's in the Pennington County jail. You and Mel will need to testify eventually. She and the other two men we arrested her with have been begging for a plea bargain. We don't need any information from them. Our investigators, thanks to Ken here, have a rock-solid foundation to build the arson and attempted murder charges."

"What about that guy, Sean Goins?" Ken asked.

Jared shrugged. "He's still in the wind, but we have a real name based on facial recognition programs. We got a good shot of him abandoning the car from a traffic camera in the area. His name isn't Sean Goins. We're waiting for him to pop up again. I don't believe he's a threat to resurface here. He's a low-level criminal. Nothing violent. Blackmail is his profession of choice."

"The guys here, they're arson investigators?" Senior nodded at the men inside and around what used to be Declan's bar.

"Yes. I flew in the best arson inspectors we had when I was informed of the fires. They're methodical and particular and won't make a call until all the evidence is analyzed. But I suspect arson charges and attempted murder charges will be filed once the facts in this case are determined. When they are, we'll be tagging them with for four counts each, arson and attempted murder."

"You'll keep us updated?" Declan wanted it to be known he wouldn't put up with any more shit from the other side of the world or just up the street. "I have a family to protect. And all the dreams of rebuilding can go to hell in a handbasket if they're in danger. I'm going to do what I need to do to protect them, which I didn't do last night." And he felt like absolute shit for that.

Jared King cocked his head and stared at him. "Declan, you were trapped inside a burning building by people who were hired to burn your livelihood down to the ground. I know that doesn't take away the sting of what could have happened. What you need to focus on, however, is what *didn't* happen. You didn't die. You could have. Your lady could be without you at this moment."

"She could be dead, too."

Jared nodded. "I'm not sure your house was a target. From the information Carrington gave me, the bar was supposed to be torched with no one inside. I'll know more after I talk to our suspects in custody. If they don't lawyer up."

"She's not stupid. I don't know about the men she was with." Ken sighed. "Then again, who would have thought she'd be a part of something like this?"

"No one," Frank said. "Can't blame you for wanting to protect your family. I trust Jared. If he says your family is safe, you can abide by that."

Declan rubbed the back of his neck. "Yeah, okay. Thank you." He looked at the rubble. "In my office is a small safe. It has last week's deposit in it."

"I'll make sure my men safeguard it until they've finished. We'll be at your place as soon as they're done here, so we can bring it out." Jared glanced at the burned-out shell. "Go home, get some sleep."

"You look like you could use some," Senior agreed.

Declan nodded and took one final sweep of what used to be his bar. His truck, which had been parked at the back of the bar, had been consumed by the fire. Mel's truck wasn't, thanks to her wetting the area around it.

"Maybe in a bit. I need to get down to see how Mel is doing. I dropped her off at the clinic as a precaution because of all the excitement last night." He carefully shook each of the men's hands with his bandaged hand. "Thank you for everything. Mr. Marshall, I'll take you up on that offer." The sooner he started rebuilding, the sooner he'd have stability for Mel and the babies.

"I'll get those documents drawn up." Frank shook his hand.

Declan made his way to Mel's truck and started it up. He'd start fresh and build the bar better. There were things he wanted to change. He put the truck into gear and headed to the clinic.

CHAPTER 22

&

*M*el sat in the front waiting room of the clinic, drinking a cup of lemon tea. To lighten the load Declan was carrying, she'd agreed to see Eden that morning even though she was sure everything was fine with the babies. Eden did the exam, and the babies were good. Mel was tired and worried about Declan, and her blood pressure was up a bit, but everyone agreed that was understandable.

Stephanie stood at the front window of the clinic. "Well, that took longer than I thought it would."

"What?" Mel asked because she wasn't going to get out of the chair to find out. She was too tired and not that curious.

Stephanie turned to her and crossed her eyes. "Edna's inbound."

Mel chuckled. She adored Edna, but that woman was in everyone's business. The door flew open, and Edna looked around, heading straight for Mel once she located her. "Are you all right? The babies? I was so worried! I called Declan's phone, but he didn't answer."

"All of us are fine, Edna, I promise." Mel patted the woman's back as she was enveloped in a massive hug.

"The bar burned down. Thank goodness Gen took you home last night. At least you were safe. I saw Declan with a bunch of fellas. Gen said not to go over because there were investigators there. Did you see the black SUV? All those antennas and such. Government people for sure." Edna rattled on as she dropped into a seat next to her. "Ciera said Scott had to pull the bars away from Declan's office. He had to be terrified."

Mel held Edna's hand, and it occurred to her that *Edna* was the one currently terrified. She leaned her head on the older woman's shoulder. "Ken asked us not to talk about what happened last night. He didn't want any talk to interfere with the investigation."

Edna patted their joined hand. "Well, that makes sense."

"Edna, would you like some tea?" Stephanie asked from the doorway where Edna had swept by her.

"Thank you, Stephanie, but no. I just wanted to make sure Mel and the babies were okay. The ladies are waiting for me back at the diner. Gen said I should wait to make sure Eden had a chance to do a check-up on you."

"Thank you for the time. It had to be hard to wait, but really, we're fine." She squeezed Edna's hand.

"Okay. All right. I'm going to go back to the diner, then. The girls are as worried as I am. Belinda was almost in tears, poor thing."

"Please let Ms. Belinda and Miss Doris know I'm fine." Mel kissed Edna's cheek. "You're so kind to worry."

"Well, you're part of this town, you know. We look out for our own." Edna sniffed a bit and made a swipe at a tear.

Mel smiled. "Well, you and the ladies are dear friends that I cherish. Thank you."

Edna sniffed again. "Friends worry about friends."

"That they do."

"I need to get back to the girls before they head this way. I'll stop by later today?"

Mel squeezed her hand. "Declan hasn't slept and has a lot to deal with today. Could you come by tomorrow? I'll show you and the ladies where I put all the baby shower gifts."

"That would be nice. We'll bring lunch."

"Perfect." Mel hugged Edna again, and the woman stood up. "See you tomorrow."

Stephanie opened the door and said goodbye to Edna. Then she shut the door and turned wide eyes toward Mel, who blinked, asking, "What?"

"How did you do that? You had that woman eating out of your hand." Stephanie looked at the door and then back again.

Mel shrugged and picked up her tea mug. "Her hand was shaking. She was terrified, and I like her and the girls. They may have a few rough edges, but they mean well." Mel laughed at Stephanie's lifted eyebrows. "Seriously, she's like the grandma I never had."

Stephanie pointed toward the door. "That woman is unlike any grandmother I've ever seen."

"She's a sweetie." Mel chuckled and took a sip of her tea.

Stephanie sat down beside her. "What happened out at the house?"

Mel sighed. "Ken really did ask me not to say anything to anyone. I wrote out a statement this morning. He made us breakfast. He's a sweet guy."

"He is now. Used to be a jerk. Actually, he still has his moments, but for the most part, he's grown into a good guy." Stephanie sighed. "Well, when you can tell me the good stuff, I expect first dibs on the intel.

"I promise." Mel looked up when the door opened again. Declan came in, dropped a kiss on her forehead, and sat beside her, carefully cradling her hand in his bandaged ones.

"The babies?" Declan wore worry on his face, and it was plain to see. The deep groves in his forehead and around his mouth aged him by ten years.

"Everyone's fine. My blood pressure is a bit high, but nothing to worry about."

Declan stared at her for a long moment, then nodded and whispered, "We're going to be okay." He lifted her hand and kissed the back of it.

She handed her tea to Stephanie and turned to him. He'd lost so much last night. So much had been ripped from his life, but nothing would remove her and the boys from his. "Not for a second did I think we wouldn't be. We have each other. That's all that matters."

"I love you," Declan said before leaning over and kissing her.

"Awww … I'm going to mist up here," Stephanie said, fanning her eyes.

Mel laughed and broke the kiss. Declan stood and offered her a hand. "It's lunchtime. The town will want an update. Let's grab a bite at the diner before we head home."

"Wait! Mel said Ken asked her not to say anything." Stephanie bounced her gaze from Mel to Declan.

"He did, and we'll avoid the things still under investigation. I want to thank Scott again." Declan yawned. "Frank Marshall offered to front the money to rebuild. My insurance investigator is a dick. Phil Granger's garage was looted. Took most of his specialty tools."

"You need special tools to work on cars?" Mel asked as Declan walked her to the door.

"You do, especially the big things like farm machinery. Steph, are you coming to lunch?"

"I'll grab Zeke as soon as he comes out of the exam room. Save us seats." Steph hugged Mel and then her brother. "I'm so thankful all of you are all right."

"Let's walk," Mel said as Declan started to guide her to the truck once they were outside. He adjusted their angle, and they started to the diner. "Edna was so worried."

"I figured she'd be over as soon as she saw me drop you off."

"She waited … or Gen made her wait, I'm not sure which."

"The latter, I bet." Declan guided her around a pothole in the street, then he stopped and helped her up the steps to the boardwalk in front of Gen's diner.

She looked back at him as he stared up at her. "What?"

"I don't want to wait to get married. Let's find a justice of the peace and get married. Now. Before the babies are born."

Mel extended her hand to him. Her heart hammered in her chest so hard she thought it would explode. "Are you sure?"

He stepped up and wrapped his arms around her, around them. "I've never been surer of anything in my life."

"Then, yes, I'll marry you whenever you find a

justice of the peace, a preacher, or an internet guru who can marry us."

Declan's face split into a wide smile. "An internet guru?"

Mel realized her mistake. "No. No ... Declan, I do not want an internet guru to marry us." She grabbed his arm. "Honestly, that's a big no. Veto. Declined."

"Ah, but that's not what you said." He laughed and tucked her hand through his arm as they walked to the diner's entrance.

"What I say and what I mean are two different things. I'm pregnant. I have pregnancy brain." She'd use any card she could at that point. That devilish gleam in Declan's eyes was trouble. But it was also good to see him smile even over something so silly.

Mel was once again surprised at the greeting she received at the diner. She hugged people she barely knew as she and Declan made it to the table in the back. Gen was there with her hot water and lemon tea bag. Declan ordered a soda.

"Give us the rundown of what happened," Tegan said from the booth he shared with Carson Schmidt.

"Phil and I have had some interest in our land.

The people who wanted to buy it thought they could burn me out and that stealing Phil's tools would put him out of business."

"They were sure wrong about that. Weren't they?" Reverend Campbell asked, and Father Murphey looked at Declan.

"I'm rebuilding." Declan nodded, and it seemed the entire population of Hollister let out a sigh of relief.

"Mr. Marshall suggested I build onto the bar this time. A big hall for dances, wedding receptions and the like. Senior suggested fourth of July parties and Christmas tree lighting celebrations. I'll make the entrance separate from the bar, so the ladies won't have to go through the bar to enter."

"Oh, I really like that idea," Belinda said and then turned bright red, ducking behind Edna to hide from the crowd at the diner.

"I'd love to see those plans," Carson agreed.

"I'm going to have them drawn up by a professional. There are a few things I want to change," Declan noted with a nod.

"Mel, I heard you were fighting the fire last night with a garden hose," Ciera said as she delivered a trayful of lunch specials. Mel's mouth watered at the sight of chicken fried steak, mashed potatoes, and mixed veggies.

"Oh, that looks good," she said before realizing she hadn't answered Ciera. "Sorry, the babies are hungry. I wasn't actually fighting the fire, but I did wet down the land in front of my truck and as far as I could around the old place. I wasn't going to lose my home. Not after all the wonderful work you did to restore it."

"Your plate is the next one up," Gen said as she weaved through the crowd at the bar and headed to the booths.

"Declan, did you tell her that, technically, that was fighting the fire." Kerry Ross laughed as he asked.

"I did. She doesn't see it that way. What can I do?" Declan shrugged his shoulders.

"Your hands are all bandaged. Did you get burned?" Allison asked from one of the booths where she sat with her mom and Kathy Prentiss.

"No. This is from trying to get out."

There was silence for a moment as Steph and Zeke walked in. "Why couldn't you get out?" Doris, one of Edna's ladies-in-waiting, asked.

Declan blinked and then looked at her. Mel knew he'd let the cat out of the bag. She put her hand on his. "The fire had gotten pretty bad. He had to look for a different way out."

"What about that fancy fire extinguisher you put in?" Doc Macy was the one to ask that time.

"Ah, well, that's another story. It wasn't charged." Declan shook his head. "No water, no chemicals, just a dry system."

"Well, hell, Declan, that don't make no sense. You mean they forgot to fill it with stuff?" Tegan gaped at him.

Declan shook his head. Their plates were put down in front of them, and Mel started to dig in. Declan made sure she had a napkin as he replied. "That's what I'm telling you."

"Do you know how it started? The fire, I mean?"

Mel thanked goodness she had a mouth full of mashed potatoes and gravy. It prevented her from blurting out that Miss Mule did it.

"Arson investigators are at the Bit now trying to piece that together," Declan answered and then shoveled in a huge bite of steak.

"Arson investigators," Edna said and leaned back, looking down the street to where the remainder of the Bit stood. "That's the people in the black SUV with all the antennas?"

Declan paused with a bite of food halfway to his mouth. "Ah, no. That's the government people."

"Government?" Edna's head snapped back toward Declan. "Why?"

"The arson people came with them. Could be they don't think the fire started by natural means." Declan shoved his mouth full of food as Mel turned to stare at him. He winked at her, and she shook her head. The way Declan baited poor Edna …

"Really?" Edna turned and looked at her cronies. "I guess we have some sleuthing to do, ladies."

Zeke shook his head and stared at Declan as his plate was set in front of him. When Corrie left, Zeke leaned across the table. "Why do you wind her up?" he whispered.

Declan smiled and nodded to the booth. The women were leaning in and whispering. "They eat it up, and it gives them something to do."

Phil Granger entered the diner with his wife, Sarah, and Mel listened as Phil was greeted in the same way. Of course, everyone wanted to hear what he had to say. It was the retelling of what Declan had already said, but the crowd lapped it up.

Mel finished her meal and looked around the little diner. The people there were wonderful. They were caring, responsible, giving, and, most importantly, friends. A sense of contentment, even through events of the last twenty-four hours, seeped into her bones. Hollister, the tiny town at the crossroads of two two-lane roads, had a heart the size of the state of South Dakota. The people were real, the friendships cemented in respect, and the hard life each lived was made a bit easier by coming together in times like these. It was where she would live the rest of her life with the man she loved and raise their family.

CHAPTER 23

*D*eclan had bowed to Melody's wishes and decided not to ask someone to get ordained online to marry them. Although, having one of his friends dress up like Elvis and marry them would make for a memorable wedding day. Instead, he, Mel, Zeke, and Stephanie were heading to Rapid to the justice of the peace. Zeke and Stephanie were driving in a separate vehicle so they could spend the weekend in the Black Hills. Eden was covering for Zeke, so the couple was taking advantage of the time off.

It had taken forever for them to get an appointment on a Friday with a judge in Pennington County. They chose Pennington because it had the most judges, and they had a better chance of getting in sooner, but that theory flatlined. Mel shifted in the seat, and his eyes immediately darted to her. "Are you okay?"

"My back is killing me." She shoved a little pillow that she carried around with her behind her back and sighed. "Better." She rubbed her stomach, which was huge. He couldn't say that out loud, or Mel would cry, but man, those kids were going to come out ready to play football or maybe needing a shave.

"What is that?" Music filled the air, and Mel looked at him. "Is that your phone?"

"Yeah, I have to change that ringtone." He didn't like classical music, but he didn't want to put it on vibrate on the off-chance Mel called him when he wasn't at the house, which seemed to me more and more lately due to all the work required to rebuild the Bit and Spur.

He pulled the phone out of the console of his truck and put it on speaker. "Hello."

"Declan, this is Jared King. Do you have a minute?"

"I do. I'm driving with Melody. We have an appointment in fifteen minutes."

Jared laughed. "Hopefully, this won't take that long. I wanted to let you know that the arson report has been forwarded to your insurance agent. It will detail, in-depth, the factors that contributed to the fire. None of which were negligence, intent, or willfulness on the part of the owner. The fire system wasn't charged. Negligence on the part of the installer. If you don't hear from Mr. Delt in a week or so, please let me know. I'd love to shake that little rat's cage."

Declan laughed. Mr. Delt seemed to have made an indelible impression on Jared. "Thank you, I'll take you up on that." He'd already accepted one check from Mr. Marshall for living expenses and to get the architect to move forward with the design of the new Bit and Spur. He didn't want to take too much, although he suspected Mr. Marshall could give Senior a run in the money department. Still, it would be better if he could do it on his own.

"Now, on to different news. Mr. Scanlon, as you know, was found guilty of the assault on Melody, but he hasn't said a word. We haven't found a way to tie him to what was happening, so we're still working on that issue. I have tabs on him, and with the other sentencing for the other crimes in New York, he won't see the light of day for at least ten years."

"What happens after ten years?" Mel asked from her side of the seat. She winced and tried to get comfortable.

"He'll be monitored, and we'll alert you if need be," Jared reassured Mel.

"And DeeDee?" Declan didn't want that woman forgotten or marginalized.

"Ah, yes. Ms. Hillier was arraigned yesterday for four counts of attempted murder and arson. The men Carrington hired flipped on her like they were flapjacks on a hot fire, as Frank would say." Jared chuckled. "She was the one who talked them into blocking the exits. She was the one who took them out to your place, and she alone wedged the metal under the doors and threw the gas on the house. She also lit the flame. All four men confirmed that fact."

Declan sighed and looked over at Mel. "Yet they went along with it."

"I didn't say they were smart, just that they'd flipped on her. They will also be charged with attempted murder and arson. However, Ms. Hillier will be facing the most serious charges. The court date has not been set. Due to the nature of the crimes, the DA requested no bail for any of them. The judge concurred. We'll assist the DA in any way they need to ensure this case is prosecuted to the fullest extent of the law. We value our relationship with Hollister."

"Thank you, but we who live in Hollister have no relationship with Guardian. Aren't they a big city organization? I'm not quite sure what you're talking about." Declan dropped the canned comment that everyone in the town seemed to use whenever anyone mentioned Guardian's name.

"And I appreciate that, too." Jared laughed.

"May I ask one question, though?" Declan asked.

"You may, and I'll answer it if I can."

"The people who backed the ones charged. Are they out of the picture, as you said?" He'd briefly told Mel about the foreigners looking for land, but he specifically didn't worry her with the thought that they might try again.

"Yes. We're firmly convinced they're not a threat," Jared acknowledged.

"Thank God." Declan grabbed Mel's hand and kissed the back of it.

"I'll keep you updated on the trial date once it's set. Depending on the experience of the public defender, the date can be manipulated and pushed back. A request can be submitted for separation of trial instead of trying them all together. Literally, it could take years to get to court."

"Years?" Melody repeated.

"Unfortunately. But the DA is well aware of my interest in this case. If anything goes sideways, I'll be the first to know, and you'll be the second," Jared reassured them.

"Thank you," Melody said.

"You're welcome. I'll call if I need to, but if you don't hear from me, everything is progressing as expected. So, no news is good news."

"I'll take it." Declan smiled at Mel as they said their goodbyes and hung up. Declan put on the blinker and turned left. "You don't look happy." He glanced at her again.

"I am. My back is killing me." Mel sighed. "I think I need to stand up."

"We're almost there. Two minutes." Declan hurried into the parking lot and found a spot. Then he hustled to her side of the truck and helped her down. "Here's Zeke and Stephanie."

Mel grimaced and pushed on her back. "That's a little better."

"Are you ready to get married?" Stephanie walked up and handed Mel a small bouquet.

"Oh, this is so sweet! Thank you." Mel buried

her nose in the carnations and roses. "They smell heavenly."

"I want white carnations and red roses for our wedding." Stephanie grabbed Zeke's arm and smiled up at him.

"I can't wait. Hopefully, I'll have my figure back by February." Mel pulled her jacket around her, but even the oversized coat wouldn't close around her belly.

"You will. You'll be surprised how your body adjusts," Zeke said as they all strolled into the courthouse at Mel's pace, which wasn't very fast.

"I just wish my back would adjust. It isn't happy with me." Lately, it seemed like Mel walked with her hand permanently affixed to her back.

"Not too long now." Stephanie tried to be encouraging, and Declan got it. When he did that, Mel would get a little snippy, but she just smiled at Stephanie.

"Eden said they needed to gain some more weight." Mel sighed. "I just don't know where they're going to put it."

"This way." Zeke pointed down the hall, following the directional arrow.

They walked down the long hallway and

entered the judge's offices. A thin woman stood up. "May I help you?"

"We have an appointment with Judge Whitmore."

"Do you have your license and ID with you?" the assistant asked politely.

Declan handed everything to her after Mel fished it out of her purse. "Perfect. The judge will be with you in just a moment." She handed their IDs back.

"Do you want to sit?" Declan was concerned about Mel. She was looking pale.

"No. Yes … I'm just not comfortable." Mel looked up at him, exasperated.

He glanced a Zeke, and the man's brow was creased. "Mel, how long has your back been hurting like this?"

"Off and on for a day or so." She grimaced and shifted.

"The judge is ready for you," the woman announced. Declan met Zeke's eyes over Mel's head.

"Mel, you could be in labor," Zeke said, stilling everyone.

"No. Nope. I'm not in labor. I'm getting

married." Mel shook her head and waddled toward the open door.

"She's in labor," Zeke told him.

"I am not," Mel yelled back.

The judge was standing behind his desk with a look of shock. "Is everything all right?"

"There's a good chance she's in labor," Zeke explained the situation with one sentence.

"Oh, well, then, let's press on with this, shall we? Mr. Howard?" He looked at Zeke.

"That's me," Declan said from beside Mel. He put his arm around her and allowed her to lean on him.

"Ms. Erikson?" He glanced at Melody.

"Yes. That's right." Mel tensed next to him.

"Good, so let's begin."

Mel leaned forward and groaned. "Oh, God."

"What?" He, Zeke, and Stephanie all reached for Mel, but Mel lifted her head.

"Judge, I think my water just broke. Please, for the love of God, cut through the bullshit and marry us."

The judge stammered for a moment and then popped off with the question, "Declan Mason Howard, do you take Melody Ann Erikson as your wife?"

He held onto Mel. Frankly, he was scared as shit at that point and figured they could go a little faster. "I do." He whipped that comment out like a winning trump in a card game. Quick and to the point. "Hurry up, man," he encouraged the judge. He saw Mel's slacks darken. Oh, hell …

"Ah … right. Melody Ann Erikson, do you take Declan Mason Howard as your husband?"

"I … ah …" Mel's hand squeezed his hard enough to cut off the blood supply. "Do. I do." She said through clenched teeth.

"I'll sign the document. Congratulations, you're married." The judge leaned forward. "I'll have my secretary file this after she calls an ambulance."

"No need for an ambulance." Zeke looked over at Declan. "We'll take her in your truck. It'll be faster. Go to the emergency room. Steph, follow in our truck, okay?"

"You bet."

Declan bent down and picked Mel up, but she tried to stop him. "I'm wet. I'll get you wet. Put me down; I can walk."

"Nope. I'm not worried." The lie of the century. Right now, he was worried about everything. He angled her through the judge's door and walked as fast as humanly possible to the exit.

Zeke pushed open the door while Stephanie darted to Zeke's truck. Zeke guided him as he approached the truck. "Declan, let's put her in the back seat."

Zeke opened the door, and Declan carefully loaded Mel into the back seat. Then Zeke got in the front seat and twisted. "Can you tell me what you're feeling right now, Mel?"

"Like I'm sitting on a picket fence," she groaned. "Declan. Drive faster."

Declan glanced over at Zeke, who nodded. It was less than five miles to the hospital, but it felt like it took forever. Every hesitation of the drivers in front of him sent him spiraling into a panic. By the time he pulled up to the emergency room doors, he was a wash of sweat. He jogged around the truck, and he and Zeke got her out and into a wheelchair that someone in scrubs pushed out of the lobby area.

Zeke rattled on with the medical lingo as he pushed the wheelchair into the hospital. Declan held Mel's hand until he was presented with a clipboard full of paperwork. He scribbled the answers as fast as he could, then Zeke held out his hand. "I'll move your truck. They're taking her straight up to labor and delivery. I'll meet you there."

He handed over his keys and hustled after the orderly pushing Mel. From then on, Declan just held onto Mel's hand. The only time they were separated was when the nurses helped her get undressed, cleaned up, and into a gown. He didn't go far and was back in the room seconds later.

"Hi, I'm Reena Bonner. I'm a nurse practitioner, and I'll do a look-see and find out where we are, okay? We're going to put a fetal monitor on you, too."

Two other women in scrubs went to work. Mel squeezed his hand again. This time his fingers went white with the constriction. "Ok, well, I don't think we're going to have time for a spinal."

"What? What's that? A spinal?" Crazy with worry, he demanded an answer.

"It's okay, dad. This baby is coming right now. The head has crowned, and she's at ten. So, we're going to deliver."

"Now?" Mel sounded as astonished as he was.

"Yep. Your medical records said twins."

"Yes, but I'm only thirty-five weeks. They need to grow."

"Ah, twins come early. How long have you been in labor?"

"Since my water broke in the judge's office?"

"Judge?" the woman asked as she removed the bottom half of the table and others scrambled around her.

"We just got married," Declan filled her in.

"Well, congratulations. Now, the next time you feel a contraction, I want you to lift her shoulders up a bit, and Mom, I need you to bear down. I'll talk you through it. Just listen to my voice. Dad, you ready?"

"I am." Lord, he so *wasn't* ready.

EPILOGUE

"This was a fantastic idea." Stephanie stared at the twinkle lights that hung from the exposed beams of the new community hall, dubbed the Saddle by Declan. She spun and laughed. "I can't believe they got it done in time."

Mel chuckled and swayed with Scott on her hip. Declan had Jared and would join them in a minute. They'd decided to name the boys after the people who'd helped them get through some very tough times. Scott Evers, who'd saved Declan's life, and Jared King, who was a strong, silent force behind the pursual of the court cases against DeeDee Hillier et al., and the insurance payout that had been stalled by one Mr. Delt.

"So, Sunday is the big day? Do you have everything ready? Is there anything I can do?"

"No, Gen and Allison have taken care of all the last-minute things. You have your dress, right?"

"Yes, and it actually fits." She'd sometimes wondered if her body would ever be the same. It wasn't, but she'd lost the weight, and keeping up with two infant boys was an aerobic exercise in itself.

"Zeke's mom is coming in three days. I've talked to her so many times over the phone. I can't wait to meet her in person." Stephanie almost floated over to her. "I'm getting married on Sunday!"

"I know." Mel laughed when Stephanie took Scott from her and made silly voices and faces, making him laugh.

Zeke and Declan walked in from the bar entrance. The doorway from the bar was tucked back and out of sight, keeping the ladies of the town happy. The bar wasn't finished, but Declan had insisted the hall be done in time for his sister's wedding. Another reason she adored her husband.

"Are you ready, babe?" Declan asked her.

"You're sure you're okay with taking the babies

tonight and tomorrow?" She asked Stephanie, knowing they could be a handful.

"Absolutely." Stephanie bounced Scott around. "I hope you two have amazing plans after court tomorrow."

Declan snorted. "Is sleeping an amazing plan?" He looked at her.

"I think so." She nodded. Sleep was something they both didn't get much of.

"Wow, you two sound like an old, gray-haired couple." Stephanie laughed.

"Wait until you have children, and then talk to me about feeling old." Declan kissed Jared and handed him over to Zeke.

"That will wait until after we're married." Zeke swayed with Jared the same way Stephanie swayed with Scott. "Unlike you, I don't want my anniversary and the baby's birthday to be the same."

"I'll have you know that was *not* planned." Mel kissed Scott while Stephanie held him, and then walked over to Zeke to kiss Jared.

"I know. I was there, remember?" Zeke laughed.

"Barely. It's all a blur." Mel joked. That day was marvelously stressful, wonderfully chaotic, and a blessing rolled into one.

"Lock up for us out here?" Declan asked Zeke.

Stephanie had a key so she could decorate and have flowers delivered.

"You got it."

"Did you get the car seats moved over?" she asked Declan as they walked into the bar area. It was enclosed and coming along nicely. The footprint was bigger, allowing for a longer bar and a pool table area, with the booths on the other wall. Declan had included into the build a U-shaped section for the dartboard to keep stray darts from finding the people in the booths.

Declan's office was not next to the storeroom. All alcohol was now stored downstairs in a big basement that would be lined with shelves to make inventory easier. The galley wash area was bigger and had storage for the racks of glasses they'd order once they got closer to opening.

"Seats are moved over. Formula, clothes, diapers, everything is all set up for them. Are you ready to go?" Declan asked her as they locked up.

She pulled her coat around her. There wasn't much snow, but it was cold. "No. But we have to do it, right?"

"We do. But that's tomorrow. Tonight, we're going to go out to dinner and then spend a night in a hotel … with no children." Declan waggled his eyebrows at her.

She got into the truck and closed the door behind her. When he was behind the wheel, she turned to him. "Declan?

"Yes, ma'am?" He smiled over at her.

"Maybe we should stop at the house before we go to Rapid."

Declan's brow furrowed. "Why? Do you feel okay?"

Melody smiled at him. "I feel wonderful. But we should stop anyway." When Declan's brow furrowed in confusion, she added, "Because there are no babies at the house."

"Oh, Mrs. Howard, I do like the way you think."

"Then drive faster," Mel stage whispered.

As soon as Declan came to a stop, Mel sprinted from the car to the house. She pulled off her coat and dropped it in the front room. Hopping on one foot, she pulled off one shoe and then the other. Her sweater was next.

She heard Declan behind her and laughed. His cold hands grabbed her by the waist on her bare skin, and she shrieked. They fell into bed laughing. Mel pushed him off her and straddled him. She took off her bra, and his cold hands zeroed in on her breasts. She laughed when he rolled and attacked her. The kisses and little nips of teeth, plus the scrape of his day-old beard, sent her nerves into overdrive. Little shockwaves jumped from one area to the next as they both fought to touch and kiss each other's exposed skin. Declan unfastened her slacks, stood up, and with one tug, they were off. His jeans were gone in the next instant.

She rolled over and lifted onto her hands and knees. He was on the bed and behind her in an instant. His cock entered her and pushed to the hilt. "Fuck, so good." She groaned as he grabbed her hips. He pulled her into him and bent over her, his chest hair brushing her back, his breath on her neck. The sensations culminated when he withdrew and thrust again. Sensory overload and explosive sex were what they did best.

"Declan, faster." She wanted him deeper and faster.

He lifted and grabbed her hips. The force of his movements pounded the headboard against the wall, and the sound reverberated through the house. Melody rode the wave of Declan's rapid-fire assault and shouted when she climaxed. She dropped to her elbows as Declan finished and collapsed under his weight when he fell forward. "Holy fuck, I'd forgotten how damn good noisy sex was."

Mel laughed as much as she could with Declan lying on top of her. "Quiet sex is fantastic, too."

"Wasn't disrespecting quiet sex. I love quiet sex," Declan panted and rolled over, pulling her with him. "Noisy is more fun."

"Only because it is so rare that we get to do it." She sighed. "I love you."

As Declan popped up on his elbow, she turned back to look at him. He dropped for a kiss. "I love you more with each passing day."

"I have something for you." Mel slid over to her side of the bed and pulled out an envelope. "I know you didn't want to know, but …"

Declan looked at the blank envelope and then at her. He lifted the flap and unfolded the paper. "What am I looking at?"

"The DNA test for the boys. You are one hundred percent their biological father." Mel watched as he read the letter again. He folded it carefully and closed his eyes. Mel swallowed hard. Had she hurt him by doing the test? "Are you … mad?"

Declan opened his eyes and cut his gaze to her. "No."

"What's going through your mind?" She leaned over, and her hair fell forward, brushing his chest. He reached up and ran his fingers through her hair.

"That I'm the most blessed man on the planet." Melody leaned down to kiss him again. She would make sure that Declan would never doubt that feeling. Never.

WOULD you like to read Ken's story? Click Here!

ALSO BY KRIS MICHAELS

Kings of the Guardian Series

Jacob: Kings of the Guardian Book 1

Joseph: Kings of the Guardian Book 2

Adam: Kings of the Guardian Book 3

Jason: Kings of the Guardian Book 4

Jared: Kings of the Guardian Book 5

Jasmine: Kings of the Guardian Book 6

Chief: The Kings of Guardian Book 7

Jewell: Kings of the Guardian Book 8

Jade: Kings of the Guardian Book 9

Justin: Kings of the Guardian Book 10

Christmas with the Kings

Drake: Kings of the Guardian Book 11

Dixon: Kings of the Guardian Book 12

Passages: The Kings of Guardian Book 13

Promises: The Kings of Guardian Book 14

The Siege: Book One, The Kings of Guardian Book 15

The Siege: Book Two, The Kings of Guardian Book 16

A Backwater Blessing: A Kings of Guardian Crossover

Novella

Montana Guardian: A Kings of Guardian Novella

Guardian Defenders Series

Gabriel

Maliki

John

Jeremiah

Frank

Creed

Sage

Bear

Guardian Security Shadow World

Anubis (Guardian Shadow World Book 1)

Asp (Guardian Shadow World Book 2)

Lycos (Guardian Shadow World Book 3)

Thanatos (Guardian Shadow World Book 4)

Tempest (Guardian Shadow World Book 5)

Smoke (Guardian Shadow World Book 6)

Reaper (Guardian Shadow World Book 7)

Phoenix (Guardian Shadow World Book 8)

Valkyrie (Guardian Shadow World Book 9)

Flack (Guardian Shadow World Book 10)

Ice (Guardian Shadow World Book 11)

Hollister (A Guardian Crossover Series)

Andrew (Hollister-Book 1)

Zeke (Hollister-Book 2)

Declan (Hollister- Book 3)

Ken (Hollister-Book 4)

Hope City

Hope City - Brock

HOPE CITY - Brody- Book 3

Hope City - Ryker - Book 5

Hope City - Killian - Book 8

Hope City - Blayze - Book 10

The Long Road Home

Season One:

My Heart's Home

Season Two:

Searching for Home (A Hollister-Guardian Crossover Novel)

Season Three:

A Home for Love

STAND ALONE NOVELS

A Heart's Desire - Stand Alone

Hot SEAL, Single Malt (SEALs in Paradise)

Hot SEAL, Savannah Nights (SEALs in Paradise)

Hot SEAL, Silent Knight (SEALs in Paradise)

ABOUT THE AUTHOR

Wall Street Journal and USA Today Bestselling Author, Kris Michaels is the alter ego of a happily married wife and mother. She writes romance, usually with characters from military and law enforcement backgrounds.

Made in the USA
Columbia, SC
29 May 2023

17294177R00157